THE STEEL PALACE

Also by Hugh Pentecost

Julian Quist Mystery Novels:

Die After Dark
Honeymoon With Death
The Judas Freak
The Beautiful Dead
The Champagne Kiler
Don't Drop Dead Tomorrow

Pierre Chambrun Mystery Novels:

The Fourteen Dilemma
Time of Terror
Bargain With Death
Walking Dead Man
Birthday, Deathday
The Deadly Joke
Girl Watcher's Funeral
The Gilded Nightmare
The Golden Trap
The Evil Men Do
The Shape of Fear
The Cannibal Who Overate

A David Cotter Mystery Novel:

Murder as Usual

THE STEEL PALACE

Hugh Pentecost

A Red Badge Novel of Suspense

DODD, MEAD & COMPANY
New York

Printed in the United States of America
by The Haddon Craftsmen, Inc., Scranton, Penna.

1 2 3 4 5 6 7 8 9 10

Library of Congress Cataloging in Publication Data

Philips, Judson Pentecost, date
The Steel Palace.

(A Red badge novel of suspense)
I. Title
PZ3.P5412St [PS3531.H442] 812'.5'2 77-14007
ISBN 0-396-07491-X

Part I

R. 5

1

It had been a day of surprises, winding up in a moment of genuine shock. Julian Quist was not a man easily surprised or shocked, but he had experienced both emotions in the last few hours. He had heard rumors about the man who faced him across the room but nothing that quite prepared him for the climax. He had been ushered into a private room at the very top of the twenty-three-story hotel overlooking the ocean to meet with one of the richest men of all time. After what he had seen in the last few hours he had anticipated, despite warnings, some sort of fabulous luxury.

"He lives very simply," Paul Calloway had said.

Quist expected something perhaps austere, but magnificient in its simplicity. He found himself, instead, in what looked—and smelled—like a garbage dump. It was a very large room, perhaps fifty feet square, littered with old newspapers, bits of food served on paper plates, and discarded, empty paper cups. An unmade bed in the corner looked as if the sheets hadn't been changed in a long time. The room was stiflingly hot, heated from vents that must have been designed for air conditioning but which poured out stale hot air in spite of a warm summer day.

The relic of a man sat in an old-fashioned Morris chair, a

board placed across the arms which served as a table, perhaps a writing desk. The man, whom Quist knew to be no more than sixty years old, looked like a decayed octogenarian. Long, greasy gray hair hung down to his shoulders and over his forehead so that his glittering black eyes were almost hidden. He wore a soiled-looking flannel bathrobe over equally soiled-looking blue pajamas. He held up a clawlike hand, fingernails a good inch or two long, as Quist started forward, after the first moment of disbelief, for the ordinary courtesy of a handshake.

"No closer than you are, please, Mr. Quist," the man said. The voice was a croaking, feeble sound.

At that moment the dark wall behind the man's chair was brilliantly illuminated. It was transparent, and behind it Quist saw a man, wearing what looked like a ski mask. This man held a high-powered rifle to his shoulder, a rifle with a telescopic sight. It was aimed directly at Quist's heart.

"I cannot run risks, Mr. Quist," the relic in the chair said. "If you come a step closer, my man will not wait for orders. Do I make myself clear?"

"Quite," Quist said.

The lights went out at the far wall, but Quist knew that the man with the rifle was still there, able to see his target quite clearly.

"A phobia about assassination," Calloway had said.

Quist had had an early indication of this phobia. In the lobby of the hotel a man, armed with a machine pistol, had been stationed outside the private elevator. In the elevator another man, wearing an obvious shoulder holster, had ridden to the penthouse level with Quist and Calloway.

"You are to go in alone," Calloway told Quist when they stepped off the elevator. "You will pass through the beam of an electric eye just before you reach the door. If you should happen to be carrying a gun, it would be most unfortunate for you."

"I'm not carrying a gun," Quist said, wishing, in spite of his curiosity, that he was back in the cool sanctuary of his Beekman Place apartment in New York.

He had stepped toward the door and it opened to admit him, operated by some hidden mechanism, controlled by an unrevealed operator. Perhaps that caricature of a man in the Morris chair had buttons or levers within reach of his clawlike hands.

"I am surrounded by conspiracy, Mr. Quist," the man in the armchair said. "I have to take every means possible, no matter how melodramatic, to protect myself. Assassinations are commonplace in today's world."

Quist took a handkerchief out of the breast pocket of his pale blue linen jacket and blotted at the sweat that had started to form on his forehead. It must be 85 degrees in this cluttered room. The windows, which Quist's sense of direction told him faced the ocean, had been boarded over, hermetically sealed. A florescent light in the ceiling provided the only illumination. Quist found himself fantasizing that he was walled into an evil-smelling tomb with a living corpse.

It wasn't believable. The day before, Quist had seen a dozen or more promotional pictures of Barney Steel. Admittedly they had been taken ten or fifteen years ago, but they had shown a tall, vigorous, athletically built man with piercing black eyes, smiling a white-toothed smile. In no more than fifteen years Barney Steel had degenerated into this wreck of a man, yellow-fanged, claw-nailed, a skeleton weighing fifty pounds less than the pictures had shown. This man, with the money to buy a whole nation if he chose, had not bothered to acquire clean pajamas, or clean sheets, or, apparently, a razor to shave his scraggly beard. His right hand rested on the drawing board in front of him, and his long nails made a scratching sound on the wood.

"You've been shown around the Palace, Mr. Quist?" Barney Steel asked.

"It's an amazing place," Quist said.

"I'm glad to hear you say so," Steel said. "I haven't seen it myself, although I approved the plans and the necessary financial outlay."

"It must have cost a small fortune."

"Fortunes are relative," Steel said. "I would guess about fifty-two million dollars." He spoke of fifty-two million dollars as though it was no more than the price of a deluxe club sandwich. "A little more than anyone else is spending down here."

Calloway had shown Quist through the Steel Palace and it was nothing short of breathtaking. Once a luxury hotel on Atlantic City's old boardwalk, it had gone to seed with the decline of that city as a vacation resort. Suddenly, with new gambling laws, Atlantic City had become a boomtown. Most notable of all the old buildings refurbished and the new buildings going up was the Steel Palace. Barney Steel had transformed the old structure into the very essence of luxury. It was to be a combination hotel, gambling-casino and entertainment center. The residence suites, individually decorated with genuine works of art, genuine Turkish rugs, expensive brocades at the windows, sunken bathtubs and glassed-in shower stalls, elaborate ice-making machines and refrigerators, were the very apex of luxury housing. The gaming rooms where roulette, blackjack, dice, and other games of chance would be played might have been transplanted from the elegance of Monte Carlo. An elaborate nightclub, tables set on a sloping floor that faced a stage large enough to present the old Ziegfield Follies, was served by a gourmet kitchen and staff. You only had to reach out to be served from glittering mahagony-topped bars by scarlet-coated waiters. The best entertainers from this country and from abroad were under contract for the next three years. There were indoor and outdoor swimming pools, sauna baths, and exercise rooms with Swedish masseurs waiting to bring jaded flesh back to life again.

"I think there is literally nothing you can ask for in this place that it can't provide," Calloway told Quist.

"Customers at three hundred dollars a day?" Quist asked.

Calloway, who looked like a conservative bank president, shrugged. "People might not pay that price for rooms," he said. "But ask them to throw their money away at roulette, or dice, or in the one-armed bandits and they will flock here to make Barney Steel richer than he already is."

"You think," Quist said.

"Barney says so, so I know so," Calloway said. "And that's why you're here, Mr. Quist—to make it *be* so. Barney likes your style."

"He doesn't know me from Adam," Quist said.

"He knows all about everyone who can ever be of any use to him," Calloway said.

Julian Quist was far from being unknown in his special field, which was public relations. The offices of Julian Quist Associates, located in a glass and steel finger pointing to the sky above Grand Central Station in New York, was a center for the creation of public images. They created public images for actors, singers, writers, politicians, big businesses, museums and art centers, airlines and vacation resorts. Around the trade, people said that one of Quist's most successful creations was the image he had made for himself. He was tall, slim, blond, with a profile that might have been lifted from a Greek coin. He wore his hair long, but carefully styled. His wardrobe, very mod in design, seemed to be endless. One's first reaction to him might have been that he was a skillful and professional show-off, probably an actor. But if you looked at him less casually you would have noticed that his pale blue eyes could take on a cold, hard light; that he was assessing shrewdly what he heard and saw. Perhaps unexpectedly, it turned out that he had a talent for listening, for drawing facts from other people rather than imposing his own glamor on them.

Paul Calloway, an executive in Barney Steel's empire, had called Quist to ask him to fly down to Atlantic City to look at the Steel Palace with the idea of promoting it. Quist hesitated, unwilling to commit himself to spending time away from his home base.

"Barney Steel will pay you a hundred thousand dollars to go down to Atlantic City and spend a day looking over the setup," Calloway said.

"You're kidding," Quist said.

"I understand that Carroll O'Connor gets a hundred grand for acting in each episode of *All In The Family,*" Calloway said. "I suggest your time is no less valuable than his."

"Meeting Barney Steel might make it worthwhile," Quist said.

Calloway's lined face seemed to belong to a tired man. "You may not get to see him," he said.

"I don't work for people I don't see," Quist said. "You may think that's eccentric in view of the fee, but that's the way I am."

"I'll see what can be arranged," Calloway said.

A couple of hours later a messenger delivered a certified check to Quist for a hundred thousand dollars, along with a note which said that Steel would see him. There was a flight to Atlantic City in one of Steel's privately owned planes.

And now Quist was seeing this ghastly remnant of a once handsome and dynamic man. Several of the pictures he'd seen the night before had shown Steel in the company of some of the most glamorous women in the social world and in the theater and films. No woman would look at this desiccated wreck in the Morris chair. Perhaps for a few million bucks? Quist had never quite believed that "every man has his price." Women? Never, he told himself. Not for what was left of Barney Steel. No price would make that worthwhile.

"Has your life ever been threatened, Mr. Quist?" Steel asked.

"Most recently about a minute ago—by your sharpshooter friend," Quist said.

"I apologize for the necessity," Steel said. His long nails scratched at the writing board in front of him. "As I told you when you first came in, I am surrounded by conspiracies. People want what I own, want to control what I own. If I were to die, a hundred men would split up the world I have put together."

"May I ask you an impertinent and very personal question, Mr. Steel?"

"You may ask. I may not answer."

"I've seen many photographs of you over the years," Quist said. "It's a shock to find you looking as you do. Are you suffering from some kind of terminal illness?"

"You could call it an illness," Steel said, in a grating voice. "It is the illness of perpetual fear for my life. I do not want to die, Mr. Quist. Too many people would like to get their hands on what I own. I get no loyalty from my associates. I buy it from three or four lesser people, people who cannot hope to inherit anything from me or acquire any part of my estate. Would you believe that I have made millionaires of the man who prepares my food, of the man behind that wall, of the two men who guard the private elevator which is the only access to this room? They will give me loyalty because their unthinkable salaries will stop the instant anyone so much as comes within ten feet of me."

"You don't trust people like Calloway?" Quist asked.

"There are a few, like Calloway, who have decided they will do better for themselves working under my orders than trying to handle my empire by themselves. But they could change their minds overnight."

"But you let me come here, knowing nothing about me. Maybe someone bribed me to get at you," Quist said.

The yellowing teeth appeared in a brief smile. "I bribed you," Steel said. "A hundred thousand dollars for one day at the Steel Palace. And I know all about you, Mr. Quist. You were born on May fifteenth, nineteen thirty-eight. You have never been married, but you have shared your apartment on Beekman Place in New York for several years with a very beautiful woman named Lydia Morton. Your closest male friend, one of your associates, is a former professional football player named Dan Garvey. You bank at the Irving Trust Company, the Forty-second Street and Park Avenue branch, just around the corner from your office. Your personal checking account contained ten thousand, eight hundred, and forty-two dollars as of this morning—before you deposited my check."

"Which went into the business account," Quist said, his smile thin and a little angry.

"Your business made a profit for you and your associates of something a little over seven hundred and fifty thousand dollars in nineteen seventy-six."

"Only my tax accountant knows that," Quist said. "Are you just making an educated guess?"

"I have ways of finding out anything in this world I need to know," Steel said.

"And you needed to know about my finances?"

"Of course. How else would I know how much to offer you for your services?" Steel said. "And I offer you one million dollars, of which the one hundred thousand you deposited this morning will be considered a down payment, non-refundable if you refuse. That is meant to be clear profit to you and your associates. I will pay all expenses you deem necessary. One promotion will make you more than your entire business did last year."

Quist laughed. "And who do I have to kill for you, Mr. Steel?"

"You have to make the Steel Palace irresistible to every rich man in the world, a gambling Mecca to which they will be drawn from every corner of the globe."

"Why have you chosen me?" Quist asked.

"Because you are the best man to be had at your business," Steel said. He sat forward in his chair.

Quist was suddenly aware that someone had come into the room, noiselessly, from behind him. He turned and saw a man in a plain dark suit carrying a tray. On the tray was a paper plate. On the paper plate were the two halves of a very small sandwich.

"Ah, Claude," Steel said. "I was beginning to wonder about you. What have we today?"

"Peanut butter and jelly, Mr. Steel," the man said.

Steel looked at Quist. "I never tire of peanut butter and jelly," he said "Ever since I was a small boy! Claude, this is Mr. Quist. He is joining our team."

Claude nodded politely.

"I haven't said I would accept your offer, Mr. Steel."

"But you will," Steel said. "I suggest you talk to Calloway. He knows exactly what I have in mind. If you'll excuse me now, I'll have my lunch." He reached out his bony hands for the peanut butter and jelly sandwich.

The elevator, operated by the gun-toting guard, whisked Quist down to the main lobby of the Steel Palace. The man waiting there with the machine pistol kept Quist covered until he got some kind of signal from the man on the elevator. Across the deserted lobby, decorated by magnificent glass chandeliers that looked as if they'd come out of a king's palace, Paul Calloway stood in the open door of an office.

From the screened windows facing the ocean, Quist took a deep breath of fresh air. He felt as if he hadn't breathed for the last half hour. He was aware that the back of his shirt was wringing wet with perspiration.

Calloway led him into a plush office with a picture window looking out toward the boardwalk. Calloway sat down behind a flat-topped desk, which didn't look as if anyone did any work at it. There was an intercom box, three telephones, red, white, and blue in color. But there were no papers or any other indication of work. Quist sat down in a big green leather armchair facing the desk, and wiped at his face with his handkerchief.

"Like everyone who gets to see him, you look shocked," Calloway said.

Quist shook his head. "You watched this happen? Surely the man is sick."

"Sick with fear," Calloway said in his tired voice. His babyish old face was slightly flushed, as if he'd had one too many martinis at lunch. "It started twelve—thirteen years ago, this phobia about assassination. Maybe a little before that when

President Kennedy was shot, although none of us was really aware of it at first. Wherever he was he wouldn't let anyone in to see him before they were searched for weapons. The anxiety grew and grew. He wouldn't eat food prepared for him away from his own kitchen without having someone else try it first. Finally even that wasn't good enough. He now has a man who makes sandwiches for him!" Calloway shook his head. "Would you believe that man makes more money than many of the top business executives in this country?"

"Steel suggested as much to me," Quist said.

"For the first ten years of this gradual disintegration he had with him a man who had been his houseman and valet for a long time. He used to be a smart dresser, you know, very particular about clothes. Mike McCormick had been with him when he was surrounded by women. Mike loved him. Finally he couldn't stand watching what was happening to Barney. He quit. Barney offered him a king's ransom to stay on but Mike wouldn't. And so Claude Dubois, who had managed a château Barney has in the south of France, was picked to succeed Mike, but not before he had been screened like someone about to be given control of the nation's atomic power! I think Barney plans to spend the rest of his life in that room upstairs. The Steel Palace is to be his final fortress."

"It isn't rational," Quist said. "Does he make sense in business?"

Calloway laughed, a mirthless sound. "He is the shrewdest, cleverest, most extraordinary man ever to handle money matters in a capitalist society. Everything he touches turns to profit, undreamed of profits. His mind is like a computer. He forgets nothing; nothing that has ever happened in thousands of transactions, no casual remark that has ever been made to him by friend or enemy. He makes decisions that involve millions and millions of dollars on the spur of the moment, without any apparent study, taking advice from no one. And those decisions are always the right ones. He is beyond belief, Mr. Quist, when it comes to business."

"And he sits up there, rotting away in that overheated garbage dump? That's beyond belief. He'd be just as safe in a clean shirt, in the sunshine, in fresh air."

"Try to convince him of it," Calloway said.

"What happened to his appetite for women?" Quist asked.

Calloway shrugged. "Who knows? Perhaps he became impotent."

"At forty-eight? He can't be more than sixty now."

"Women he once was interested in have tried to see him," Calloway said. "Maybe because they cared for him, maybe because they hoped to get some kind of financial help or payoff. He shut the door cold on everyone after Mike McCormick left him."

Quist was silent for a moment. "What does he have in mind in the way of my working for him?" he asked finally.

Lydia Morton, dark, sultry, with a marvelous figure, looked like a high-fashion model rather than the brilliant researcher and writer she was for Julian Quist Associates. She was far more to Quist than a business partner. For several years now, though she kept an apartment of her own a few blocks away, she had lived with Quist in his Beekman Place duplex. They were two people deeply in love, sensitive to each other's moods and needs, sexually perfectly tuned to each other. They had never considered marriage. Why change a relationship that was already perfect? They had no secrets from each other. They were so closely tuned to each other that secrets would have been impossible.

Lydia, wearing a pale yellow housecoat, her dark hair hanging loosely down to her shoulders, greeted Quist as he let himself into their apartment on his return from Atlantic City. They didn't need words. He put down the two attaché cases and the briefcase he was carrying and held her in his arms for a moment. She knew, without any word from him, that he was troubled about something. He would tell her what it was when the right moment came.

"Bourbon?"

"A double," he said. He took off his blue jacket and draped it over the back of the couch. Then he walked out onto the terrace which overlooked the East River. The city's brilliant lights seemed to dim a sky full of summer stars. The running lights of a barge on the river moved slowly south toward the tip of Manhattan Island. Quist sat down in a comfortable wicker armchair, closed his eyes, and pressed the tips of his fingers against the lids.

"Rough time?" Lydia asked. She was standing beside him, holding the outsized old-fashioned glass that contained his drink—bourbon on the rocks. He took it from her, and his fingers touched her cool hand for a moment.

"I love you," he said.

She bent down and brushed her lips against his hair. "I missed you," she said. "You saw the great man?"

"Oh my God!" he said. He drank almost half his drink in one long swallow. "You got the strength to bring those cases out here?"

She brought the two attaché cases and the briefcase and put them on the table beside him. He opened them and revealed stacks of photographs and papers. There were the few early photographs of Barney Steel, and many new photographs of the Steel Palace.

"Take a look," he said.

Lydia began to look through the pictures, while Quist took a pad from his briefcase. He began to sketch something on it. He was an accomplished caricaturist, and what emerged was a grotesque drawing of Barney Steel today, sitting in his Morris chair, a clawlike hand held up in a stopping gesture. In the background was the man in the ski mask with the high-powered rifle.

Lydia murmured some words of disbelief as she looked at the pictures of the Steel Palace.

"It's like some fairy story dream palace," she said.

"It's to open in two weeks," Quist said. "We are supposed to sell it big in that time. Right now the staff, the various crews, are going through repeated dry runs of all the services they'll offer."

"Can anybody afford to patronize it?" Lydia asked.

"The kind of people they want to attract can," Quist said. "The very rich with gambling in their blood. Take a look at the pictures of Barney Steel. They're all ten or fifteen years old. He's now sixty."

Lydia shuffled through the pictures. "He had more than money to attract women," Lydia said.

Quist held out the pad on which he'd been sketching. "That's how he looks today," he said.

Lydia stared at the sketch and then at Quist. "You're kidding!"

"I made him look better than he does. You can't smell filth and decay in the drawing."

"Who's the man with the gun?"

"A millionaire bodyguard," Quist said. "Steel stopped me from getting any closer to him. The man with the gun made his point."

"It's weird, Julian! How could the man have disintegrated like that?"

"Fear. Fear of being murdered—they say," Quist said.

"They say?"

"Look at that picture of Steel dancing with some glamor gal. It says it was at an inaugural ball for President Johnson. That would make it nineteen sixty-five."

In the picture Barney Steel was facing the camera, smiling down at a girl in a backless evening gown. His right hand rested against the girl's bare flesh, guiding her.

"Now look at my sketch," Quist said.

"There's no way to connect them," Lydia said, after a moment's study. "A handsome vigorous man, and that—that skeleton!"

"Look closely, luv," Quist said. His voice sounded suddenly tense with a kind of excitement. "Look closely at that guiding hand against the lady's back."

Lydia frowned at the photograph. "His little finger seems to be missing at the middle joint," she said.

"Now look at my sketch. Same hand, you understand."

"In your sketch the little finger is all there," Lydia said. She looked at Quist, her eyes widening.

He took the sketch from her and tossed it down on the table along with the rest of the pictures. "It took me a long time to see it," he said. "I was going through the pictures coming back on the plane. Then I noticed. And if you look at some of those earlier pictures, you'll see it again, less obvious. The little finger of his right hand is missing at the middle joint. It isn't a piece of photographic foolery. His finger isn't doubled under as he guides his dancing partner. The other pictures make that clear." He brought his hands down on the arms of the wicker chair. "Listen, luv. The man I saw in Atlantic City, the man who offered us a million dollars clear to do a job for him, wasn't Barney Steel."

"A stand-in," Lydia said. "If he's so afraid of assassination, Steel might use a stand-in to interview strangers."

"Oh, he was a stand-in all right," Quist said. "But I've been asking myself a question for the last hour, Lydia. Is he a stand-in for a living Barney Steel or a dead Barney Steel?"

2

Dan Garvey was the direct opposite of Quist in coloring. His hair was raven-black, cut almost army-short. His early goal in life had been to be a professional football star, and for two seasons, after a brilliant college career, he had ripped the National Football League apart as a running back. Then a knee injury had put an abrupt finish to that. At loose ends, doing some sports broadcasting for one of the TV networks, Garvey had met Julian Quist at a party somewhere. The two men, so different in type and style, had taken an instant liking to each other. Quist had undertaken to promote a big new sports arena on Long Island and he decided Garvey was just the man to handle the account. Presently, after accepting the offer, Garvey was invited to become one of the associates, or partners, along with Lydia Morton and Bobby Hilliard, who looked like a young Jimmy Stewart and had a genius for dealing with explosive temperaments.

The only bad moment Garvey had ever had with Quist was right at the beginning. Garvey had gotten one look at Lydia and decided she was for him. It was made apparent to him, rather abruptly, that there was nothing doing. Lydia belonged to Quist, and vice versa.

A few days after this encounter Garvey had walked into

Quist's very mod office, modern paintings, modern furniture, a chromium-trimmed bar on wheels, where Quist and Lydia were discussing some project.

"I considered quitting," Garvey said. "I considered joining the Foreign Legion. I'd like to stay on, with the rules understood."

"There are no rules," Quist said, smiling. "Only no hope—I hope."

And so a warm and very solid relationship began. Garvey was a great man to have in your corner when the going got tough. He often disagreed with Quist, but when a decision was made by the group, Garvey played his part to the hilt. He disagreed with Quist the morning after the trip to Atlantic City.

The four partners, Quist, Lydia, Garvey, and Bobby Hilliard were gathered in Quist's office along with Connie Parmalee, Quist's secretary, a girl with red hair, hazel eyes hidden behind tinted granny glasses, and rather spectacular long legs. This was what Quist called his "family."

"My advice," Garvey said, "is that you call Calloway and tell him we've decided not to take the job. You can give him back the hundred grand, if your conscience bothers you."

"And lose the chance to make a million in profit on one two-week job?" Quist asked, giving his friend a tight little smile.

"Don't play games with us, chum," Garvey said. "It's not the money that's irresistible to you. You want to stick your head into the Steel Palace's shredding machine. You're not playing with children down there. You try to blow whatever their game is, and whatever is left of you will go out to sea in the garbage barge."

"A million dollars is a lot to give you," Bobby Hilliard said in his shy young Jimmy Stewart voice. "Can't we just do what we're hired to do, Julian, and leave their game alone?"

"Fat chance!" Garvey said, before Quist could answer. "Julian would never in God's world stay away from the cheese in the trap!"

"We may be dealing with a murder that's been committed or a murder that will be committed," Quist said.

"And it's none of our business," Garvey said. He turned impatiently to Lydia. "Don't you want your guy kept in one piece, lady?"

"You think it's that dangerous, Dan?" she asked. Her lovely face was clouded.

He turned to her with the elaborate patience of a parent trying to deal with a not very bright child. "Let me lay it out for you—for all of you," he said. "Barney Steel's empire represents God knows how many billions of dollars' worth of capital investments, and God knows how many millions of dollars' worth of annual profits. It represents oil, steel, air lines, hotel chains, shipping, coal, who knows what else! They buy and sell governments, perhaps our own! Barney Steel has been the magic man from the very beginning. Let him disappear and stockholders will rush to unload, governments will totter, the competition will move in. The men surrounding Barney Steel cannot afford to have anything happen to him. They can't even afford to let him die a natural death. So something has happened to him. Maybe he has died. Maybe he has been murdered, as Julian suggests. Maybe he's had a stroke. But it's going to be kept a secret for just as long as they can manage it. Maybe he's disintegrated into a jibbering idiot. He must have fallen apart physically or this stand-in wouldn't be playing the role he is."

"Perhaps he is in that room one day and the stand-in the next," Quist said.

"So our golden-haired hero from Madison Avenue tries to

uncover the secret, whatever it is," Garvey said. "They're not going to let you get away with it, no matter how far they have to go to stop you."

"Why bring him into it in the first place?" Bobby Hilliard asked.

"Because they want a job done that he can do better than anyone else. They don't know he's as insatiably curious as Kipling's elephant child," Garvey said. "And he'll get more than his nose pulled for sticking it into their business."

"There's something monstrous going on there," Quist said, a faraway look in his eyes. He had taken one of the long, thin cigars from the cedar-lined box on his desk, but he didn't light it.

"So call the cops and forget the job!" Garvey said.

"Is it against the law for them to have a stand-in for Steel in an interview with Julian?" Bobby Hilliard asked.

"Not when they get through explaining it," Garvey said. "And after that they'll make damn sure Julian doesn't stir up any more hornets' nests. He gets run over by a taxi or falls off his terrace at the apartment or just plain gets shot between the eyes by a sniper on a street corner."

"I think," Quist said very quietly, after a moment of silence, "I'd like to agree to do their job for them. And I promise you all not to light a fuse until I know exactly what I'm blowing up."

"Why risk it, Julian?" Lydia asked. She knew there was no point in arguing with him.

"A man may be in hell somewhere," Quist said, "surrounded by his enemies. I may be the only person who suspects it. At least I may be the only person who suspects it and may be willing to help him."

* * *

They all knew the vote was three to one against taking the Steel Palace job, and they all knew that Quist's one vote had carried the day.

"So what's for real about the job?" Garvey asked. He had surrendered. There was never any question about his going along with Quist's decision.

"They plan to open two weeks from today," Quist said. He switched on the tape recorder on his desk. Connie Parmalee would transcribe the business part of the conversation later. "We are concerned first with that opening. There are six hundred suites in the Palace. Steel means the first guests to be invited. The whole weekend will be on the house, except what is taken in at the gambling tables, and wheels, and slot machines. Rooms free, food free, liquor free, nightclub entertainment free."

"There goes another million bucks!" Garvey said.

"A conservative estimate," Quist said. "Absurdly conservative if we take our fee into account. The guest list is the important thing. They have about three hundred names involving the richest people in the world. They want us to add another three or four hundred names. Some people will decline, but not too many if we do the job right."

"It sounds like it might just be the biggest party ever given by anyone," Lydia said. Her mind wasn't quite on it. She was thinking of Garvey's warnings.

"Our job is to persuade the right people to accept Steel's invitation and to make certain that the whole world watches them troop into the Palace two weeks from now. I have their list of names." Quist picked up a sheet of paper from his desk.

"Compiling a list of rich suckers may not be as simple as it sounds," Garvey said. "Steel will pay traveling expenses from anywhere?"

"From anywhere and back," Quist said. "That means China, India, Africa, anywhere. The oil tycoons from the Middle East should make interesting targets. Let me tell you something about their list. Those three hundred names are of people who have to come, people who are obligated to Barney Steel and his multinational powerhouse. The people we are to find have to be persuaded."

"So if they don't have a full house?" Bobby Hilliard asked.

"We will have dropped the ball and they'll be very, very unhappy," Quist said.

"This seems to me to be something that should take a year to plan," Lydia said. "Two weeks doesn't give us time to turn around."

Quist leaned back in his chair, smiling. "Would you believe that Barney Steel, the financial wizard of all time, decides by the stars? He's an astrology bug. The house astrologer has told him that a propitious time to open the Steel Palace is two weeks from yesterday."

"Steel really believes that stuff?" Garvey asked.

"He believes it, or he chooses to let people think he believes it," Quist said. "The fact is that it works for him."

"The stars, or his own genius?" Lydia asked.

Quist shrugged. "You pays your money and you makes your choice," he said. "We have two weeks in which to augment his list and persuade people to come. He guarantees us a million dollars in clear profit because he thinks we can do it."

"Do we begin with Dun and Bradstreet's financial listings?" Connie Parmalee asked.

"One starting point," Quist said. "But there must be four or five people we've done business with who can give us a head-start on who is really loaded, who would like to please Barney Steel. Don't forget, pleasing Barney Steel Enterprises means more than getting silk sheets and free caviar and champagne. It means getting important, perhaps crucial, business favors. Someone we know, somewhere, must be able to draw us a map of who needs favors from Barney Steel."

"And while we go about this little job," Garvey said, the combative edge back in his voice, "what the hell are you going to be up to, Maestro?"

Quist leaned back in his chair, eyes raised to some point in the corner of the room, avoiding Garvey's straight stare. "Somewhere, some place, there is a man named Mike McCormick who was, for many years, Barney Steel's valet and, I suspect, a kind of confidant. He quit two years ago, not able to watch the terrible disintegration of the man he had served so long. That according to Paul Calloway. Also, according to Calloway, Steel pleaded with McCormick to stay on. When he wouldn't, Steel retired him as a millionaire. Steel hands out million dollar gratuities like you hand a half a dollar to a hatcheck girl."

"It's at least a dollar in any decent place," Garvey said, "as you'd know if you ever wore a hat."

"McCormick, I'm led to believe, was loyal to Steel, must have cared for him to be so distressed by his decline. If I could find him and talk to him. . . ." Quist shrugged. "Maybe he quit because Steel was no longer the man he served so long. Maybe he quit because Steel, quite literally, was no longer the man he'd served so long; was another man, a stand-in."

"With a whole finger," Garvey said.

"Wouldn't Calloway tell you where to find McCormick?" Lydia asked.

"Why do I want to see McCormick?" Quist asked. "Because I suspect something? That would put an end to the game before I got started."

"You think Calloway's in on whatever's happening?" Garvey asked.

"I don't know what I think—yet," Quist said.

"McCormick could quite simply have been bought off when the time came to substitute someone for the real Barney Steel," Garvey said. "He could no longer help Steel, his friend. A lavish retirement fund would make it worthwhile for him to keep his mouth shut."

Quist nodded. "It could be that way," he said.

"So you find him, talk to him, and he promptly gets in touch with the powers that be to warn them that you're on to something."

"It's a risk," Quist said. "The problem is to find him without stirring up a storm before I ever get the chance to talk to him."

"For God sake, why don't you forget the whole thing?" Garvey said.

"It's an itch I've got to scratch," Quist said.

The Purple Slipper is what is called in the trade an "intimate room." It can accommodate only about a hundred people at most, at about thirty-five candle-lit tables facing a small stage on which many of the top nightclub entertainers have performed over the years. It is not a room for noisy comics. Diana Lewis's low, husky voice was perfectly suited to the Slipper. She sang, holding a hand microphone as though she was making love to it. Her material was unique, part witty, part sentimental, Diana was now in her fifties but still a very beautiful woman in a theatrical way. She had a flare for stunning clothes, and a gift for holding an audience in the palms of her slender hands. Some years ago Quist had thought of her as a young Marlene Dietrich.

Like many people in show business, Diana had had her ups

and downs. A musical comedy star who had lighted Broadway for many seasons, there had come a time when she could no longer command a stage full of young people. She faded from view, remembered with affection, but no longer in the spotlight for stars. Quist had a weakness for show people who had gone off the rails. It was he who had guided Diana to the intimate one-woman thing that she now did with such consummate skill. He wasn't a talent agent. It had been a labor of love for him with no special financial reward. Now he wanted payment of another kind and he had brought Lydia to the Purple Slipper the evening of the day he had made up his mind about the Steel Palace job.

Quist and Lydia, an unusually handsome couple, sat at a corner table listening to the enthusiastic applause for Diana as she finished her midnight show. Diana came down off the stage and threaded her way between the tables to where her friends watched.

"My God, don't you two ever grow any older?" Diana asked as she reached them.

Quist stood up and held a chair for her. "That's our main aim in life, ma'am," he said.

"You both look disgustingly marvelous," Diana said. Up close you could see little wrinkles at her throat, and lines at the corners of her generous mouth that weren't visible on stage.

"Drink?" Quist asked.

"On the wagon, alas," Diana said. "Booze does bad things to whatever is left of my voice."

"You sound just tremendous," Lydia said.

"If I could just look like you, love, I wouldn't care about the sound," Diana said. "I will have a Tom Collins without the gin, if you can afford it, Julian. How nice of you both to drop by."

"You were on my mind through an odd circumstance," Quist

said, sitting down again and beckoning a waiter. "I spent some time yesterday with an old friend of yours."

"I'm glad I have friends," Diana said. "Who was it?"

"Barney Steel," Quist said.

There was a little twitch at the corner of Diana's mouth. "My God!" she said. "I'd heard he didn't see people any more."

"He wants me for a job," Quist said.

"I read in the paper he's opening some kind of gambling casino in Atlantic City," Diana said. "Hiring entertainers. Did he—did he mention me, Julian?"

"No," Quist said. "We didn't get to talking about people."

"I—I've heard he isn't well. Isn't like he used to be."

"He's gone to seed some," Quist said, the understatement of all time. "Do you mind talking about him, Diana?"

A little shudder moved Diana's bare shoulders. She was wearing an evening dress held up somehow by magic and not straps. "Old wounds have a way of never healing," she said. "I go for weeks without ever thinking about him, then you mention him and a ghost walks over my grave."

"You were fond of him?" Lydia asked, as though she hadn't known.

"I lived with him—or should I say I was kept by him—for three years." Diana's smile was mischievous. "I confess that to you, love, because you will understand. You've lived with Julian for longer than that, haven't you?"

"Happily," Lydia said.

"The difference is that Julian, I suspect, is moderately normal," Diana said. "He's not rich enough to love money more than he loves you."

"Lydia makes me richer than most men ever get," Quist said. He reached out and covered Lydia's hand with his.

"You didn't go to bed with him for money," Diana said, still addressing herself to Lydia. "I sold myself to Barney for unimaginable luxury, and I thought security. The trouble was I fell in love with him along the way."

"That was trouble?" Lydia asked.

"He would stop in the middle of lovemaking to phone someone in Cairo about a business deal," Diana said. There was bitterness in her husky voice. "He would buy me a diamond necklace afterwards to make up for it. But once I was in love with him, that didn't make up for being left high and dry!"

"And when it was over he left you without support or help?" Quist asked.

"I was responsible for that, not Barney," Diana said. "He offered to settle a small fortune on me. I turned him down. If he didn't want me, I didn't want his help. Have you ever thought of me as a romantic, Julian?"

"I've thought of you as a very special person," Quist said.

"Flattery will get you almost anything," Diana said, smiling at him. "You want to know something particular about Barney. What is it?"

"He's shut himself away in his Steel Palace in Atlantic City," Quist said. "He seems obsessed with the idea that someone is going to try to kill him. Was that always a fear of his?"

"It was growing on him," Diana said. "At first it was enough to have a bodyguard. Then he began to insist on staying hidden. Where he was had to be a secret, closely kept. He began to distrust his closest associates. Finally he began to distrust me."

"You?" Quist said, his eyebrows raised.

"I had sold myself once for money—to him," she said. "He began to be afraid I might sell myself to someone else—for love. I was the closest person to him, and I could betray him."

"He really is off his rocker!" Quist said. "Didn't the stars tell him you were safe?"

Diana sipped the lemonade drink the waiter had brought her. "He doesn't believe in the stars, Julian. He just uses them to stop arguments. I don't think anyone can understand what so much wealth and power can do to a man, particularly if he started out being a reasonably nice, normal guy," she said. "Barney made it all on his own, you know. He's a genius when it comes to money. A wizard. But I guess you don't accumulate all that money and all that power without hurting people along the way. Because Barney is a decent guy at heart, he feels guilty about what he's done to people. And eventually he convinced himself that he'd be punished for it. That's when he began to be certain that someone would try to knock him off." She shook her head. "You make a killing, Julian, and you might buy yourself a Rolls-Royce. When Barney makes a killing, he finds he's bought himself a whole country, a whole government, people who secretly hate him."

"There have been other women in his life," Quist suggested.

"Oh, Barney was a womanizer when he was young. And he was so rich so young that he could get almost anyone he wanted. He had charm, too, you know. There were movie stars, and real royalty, and other men's wives! But I was unique." Her laugh hid pain. "I was the only woman he ever stayed with for any length of time. Three wonderful, awful, frightening years."

"Was there no one he cared for besides you?" Quist asked. "No real friend he trusted?"

"Not in my time—which was when he was really hitting the top. Except Mike."

"Mike McCormick?"

"You know about him? Poor Mike. He really loved Barney. He did everything for Barney, from cutting his hair and shaving him, to cleaning up after him, guarding him, cooking for him. He was a servant, a slave, but he was paid a king's ransom for doing the job. I was astonished when he came to see me a couple of years ago and told me that he'd left Barney. 'He isn't the same any more,' Mike told me. 'I just can't work for the person he's become.' Barney begged him to stay, but Mike wouldn't. Barney fixed him financially for life, but the friendship, so valuable to both of them, was ended."

"I'd like to talk to McCormick," Quist said. "Have you any idea where he can be found?"

"I don't know, Julian. He had no plans when I saw him, except to find himself some kind of permanent place."

"I had a chance to look at a lot of early pictures of Barney," Quist said. "I was intrigued by the amputated finger on his right hand. I wondered why he'd never had some kind of cosmetic repair job done on it."

Diana smiled. "He was proud of it," she said. "He was a fighter pilot in Korea in his middle thirties. The richest pilot in the history of the air force, I imagine. He had that finger shot off in a dog fight with a North Korean pilot. He got his man, of course. He always gets his man. He used to call that finger his medal of honor. He wouldn't have dreamed of hiding it or covering it up."

Quist reached for his drink. The man he had seen in the Steel Palace was surely not Barney Steel.

"Do you think you could persuade Barney to see me?" Diana asked. "I—I'd like him to know that I—I still care for him, am concerned for him."

"I don't think there's the slightest chance he'd agree to that," Quist said.

He wouldn't agree because she would spot him in an instance for a phony.

3

It was mid-morning of the next day.

Quist had gone directly from his own apartment to the office of his friend, Lieutenant Mark Kreevich of Manhattan Homicide at police headquarters. Kreevich was a slim, wiry man with a boyish face and an intense manner. He was a new breed of cop, college educated, with a law degree. He was a man dedicated to the preservation of law and order, not the cheap "law and order" of the politicians bent on making a show for their constituents, but a law and order that should be part of a way of life. He believed that there should be a modern society in which a man could live some other way than on the defensive. You could spend an evening with Kreevich discussing art, or music, or literature, or politics, but you would be aware that his real preoccupation was with how to make his world a better place to live in.

Kreevich and Quist were old friends. Their tastes were so much alike, their mutual hatred for violence so strong, that they were naturally drawn to each other, sensitive to each other's reactions, trusting each other totally.

Quist had called Kreevich at breakfast time asking a favor. Was there any way Kreevich could trace the whereabouts of

Mike McCormick? Kreevich thought he might, but when Quist reached his office he was still waiting for answers. So Quist told him about the Steel Palace and the stand-in while they waited for a report from someone Kreevich had put on McCormick's trail.

Kreevich listened to his friend, amusement reflected in his dark eyes. "I sometimes think you are devoted to looking for trouble," he said.

"You like the sound of it?" Quist asked.

Kreevich sipped from a china mug of coffee. "You're dreaming of conspiracy and murder without a shred of evidence to go on," he said.

"The man I saw isn't Barney Steel," Quist said.

"So what? You insisted on seeing Steel. Steel doesn't see anyone, so somebody sat in for him."

"Somebody who was set up to sit in for me or anyone else who wanted to see Steel. The impersonation was far too elaborate to be a one shot."

"You expect anything to be anything but elaborate in the Steel complex?" Kreevich asked. "You've got a man with a phobia about violence. He won't see strangers. A stand-in sees you. He may have half a dozen other stand-ins for all you know. For God sake, Julian, a transparent panel with a gunman behind it? For all you know the real Barney Steel may have been sitting behind some other panel in that room, listening to every word spoken by you and the stand-in. It's melodrama, but Barney Steel has lived with melodrama all his life. He probably thrives in a world of industrial spies and counterspies. He tries to hide where he is. He sends one of his stand-ins on an open trip to Mexico, fooling reporters and friends and enemies while he stays in a hotel room in Chicago, or Los Angeles, or here in New York. This kind of subterfuge goes on all the time in a power world like Barney Steel's. I think you're overreacting, Julian."

"But suppose Steel is dead, or a prisoner of his own associates?" Quist persisted.

"So it's a game that doesn't involve you, chum. You're asked to do something quite legitimate that will make a million dollars in profits for your business. So compile your list of guests for the grand opening, collect your fee, and let the Steel empire worry about Barney Steel." Kreevich put down his coffee mug and laughed, a short, mirthless laugh. "You won't, of course, but you asked for advice."

"Is there some way, officially, that the police could insist on seeing Barney Steel?" Quist asked.

"If you mean me, I have no jurisdiction in New Jersey. Since you're going to ignore my advice, and Dan Garvey's, and, presumably, Lydia's wishes—since she cares about your survival—then let me give you another kind of advice."

"Shoot."

"Let Steel's people know for a moment that you suspect something—and if there is something to suspect—you'll be lucky if all that happens to you is that you get fired. A lot of people would think losing a million dollars' profit was a disaster. I think being dead would be a bigger disaster."

"You admit, then, that these people are capable of murder?"

"Of course I admit it," Kreevich said. "I wouldn't kill a man to steal a loaf of bread. But would I kill a man to protect everything I own? I might. And if what I owned was half the world—?" Kreevich shrugged. "When the stakes are that high, chum, a single life is small change. Get in their way and they'll swat you dead with no more compunction than they'd feel for a winter fly on a window pane. And you know why they won't hesitate? Because they are equipped to get away with it. They can hide crime. They can buy safety—and silence!"

Whatever Quist might have said at that moment was interrupted by the entrance of a uniformed policewoman from the outer offices.

"Sergeant Duane—Mr. Quist," Kreevich said.

Sergeant Duane, a rather attractive young woman, acknowledged the introduction with a crisp nod of her blond head. "The information on Michael McCormick, Lieutenant," she said. She put a piece of paper down on Kreevich's desk and took off.

Kreevich picked up the paper. "Your Mike McCormick bought himself a co-op apartment on Sutton Place," he said. "He has an unlisted phone. The number is here." He handed the paper to Quist. "My final piece of advice to a mule-headed friend. McCormick was a long-time and loyal servant of Steel's. He may know all about the stand-in or stand-ins and tell you nothing. He's apparently quite well off and indebted to Steel for that. He will play the game Steel's way, I have to assume. You start asking curious questions and he will almost certainly let Steel know."

"If Steel is alive, or if it's possible to get to him," Quist said.

"When you get an idea," Kreevich said, "you're like a terrier with a bone!"

Quist seemed not to hear. "If Steel is alive and well—relatively well—he surely can't be too annoyed at me for being concerned about him. He could warn me not to spread the rumor, assure me that he's all right. Why should he want to swat me like a winter fly, to quote you, for being concerned?"

"But if he isn't alive and well, or if he is a prisoner in the hands of his own people, those people are going to come down on you like a ton of bricks!"

"So you admit something may be cooking?"

"You're hopeless, chum," Kreevich said. He watched Quist head for the door and then stopped him. "Julian!"

Quist turned.

"If you get into some kind of trouble, shout," Kreevich said.

"Thanks, Mark. I may need you."

"Don't wait too long," Kreevich said.

Mike McCormick had chosen an expensive building on Sutton Place in which to live out his life. Why not, Quist thought as he tried to reach his man on the house phone, if he had been left as well off as both Calloway and Diana Lewis had implied? There was a doorman in uniform, a uniformed attendant in the lobby, and operators on four elevators at the rear. This was not a building where elderly tenants could be followed, pushed into their apartments, and subjected to violent attack by crime-minded teenagers. Even Quist's call from the lobby had to go through a hidden switchboard operator.

"Yes?" It was an old voice, a tired voice that came over the line.

"Mr. McCormick? My name is Julian Quist. You may or may not have heard of me. I'm in the public relations business. I'm doing a job for Barney Steel and I thought you might be willing to help me."

There was a long silence. Then: "I've heard of you, Mr. Quist."

"Would it be convenient for you to talk to me for a few minutes?"

"How did you locate me, Mr. Quist? I'm not in the phone book. So far as I know Mr. Steel doesn't know where I live."

"This is a very small city, Mr. McCormick, if you have the right contacts. May I come up?"

"I suppose you can," McCormick said.

Obviously that conversation had been monitored by the switchboard. The lobby attendant was at Quist's elbow as he turned away from the house phone.

"Apartment Twelve C," the man said. He gave some kind of hand signal to the elevator operator standing outside a waiting lift.

The man who opened the door of 12C was short, gray-haired, with heavy-lidded eyes. He was not what you might have expected in this building. He wore wrinkled slacks, a gray cardigan sweater, buttoned halfway down, and brown felt bedroom slippers.

"Come in, Mr. Quist," he said.

The living room in which Quist found himself was barely furnished. Quist had the feeling that the couch, the two overstuffed chairs, the table with a reading lamp on it had come out of a second-hand shop somewhere. Mike McCormick hadn't spent his money on luxury.

McCormick indicated one of the armchairs and asked Quist if he'd care for coffee. He poured from a battered percolator plugged into a baseboard socket. The china cup was nicked and cracked.

"I'm afraid I take it black," McCormick said. "There's no sugar or cream."

"I take it straight," Quist said. He tried his warmest smile. "You say you've heard of me, Mr. McCormick?"

"Barney talked of you quite often," McCormick said.

"Oh?"

"He considered hiring you for several different projects, but he decided against it. I wondered why he'd changed his mind about you. That's why I agreed to talk to you. I wondered."

"Why did he decide against me in the past?" Quist asked.

"He said you were a man with a too active curiosity,"

McCormick said. "He said you would be inclined to pry into things which were none of your business."

Quist suppressed an impulse to laugh. Perhaps Barney Steel had been right about him.

"I imagine," McCormick said, "that he's hired you to promote his Atlantic City gambling casino. That's a pretty wide-open venture, I'd say. Perhaps Barney figured there weren't too many secrets lying around that might interest a curious man. There's one thing about Barney, Mr. Quist. Anything he operates *he* operates. You think about gambling and you think about organized crime. He doesn't need their muscle and he doesn't need their money. It'll be a straight up-and-up operation. The wheels won't be tilted and the dealers will be on the level. Barney is a ruthless man but he isn't a thief."

"You had a long association with him," Quist said.

"We grew up together," McCormick said. "Kids on the same block—in Brooklyn, for God sake. Barney went up like a rocket when he was just past twenty and I hung onto his coattails."

"It's none of my business," Quist said, "but how does it happen that you wound up being his valet, his servant? I would have expected you to be president of a big company, part of the power structure."

"No taste for it," McCormick said. "Power is a lonely kind of climate. Barney found that out early. Everybody sucked around him for money, or influence, or whatever he had they wanted. He had no real friends, no one he could really trust—except the kid from down the block in Brooklyn. He kept me around, just so there'd be someone he could level with, let his hair down with. You understand?"

"I think so."

"Mind you, I wasn't president of a company, but Barney paid me a hundred grand a year just to be around when he needed me. That was pure gravy, you understand. I didn't have any rent to pay. I lived with Barney. I didn't have to buy food or pay traveling expenses. I didn't even have to pay for a Coke if I was thirsty. Most company presidents aren't that well off."

"But in the end you were a kind of body servant," Quist said. "Diana Lewis told me you cut his hair, shaved him, did a dozen menial chores."

McCormick lifted his heavy lids. "He was my friend. I did anything he needed from me."

"But you finally threw in the towel."

"Why are you interested, Mr. Quist?"

"Because I saw Steel day before yesterday and I couldn't believe what I saw."

McCormick put his coffee cup down and it rattled in the saucer. His hand wasn't steady. "Then you may understand why I couldn't go on any longer. Watching Barney build his empire over the years was an exciting thing. Every day was exciting. But then—well, he began to develop a neurosis, a psychosis, about assassins, about conspiracies to do him in, steal what he had. He shut himself away from the whole damned world—except me. There were armed guards behind every door, behind every panel. He show you his man with the machine pistol?"

"Yes."

"He had been a man who was proud of his physical appearance, vain about his clothes, his attractiveness to women. Gradually he became an unwashed, unshaved, uncared for madman. Oh, he still has a genius for handling his money, his businesses, but he stopped being anything like a normal person. He wasn't the man I'd spent thirty-five years serving. I couldn't take it any more."

"But if he was in big trouble, would you respond to a call for help from him?" Quist asked. His impulse was to trust this man in spite of Garvey's warnings.

"Not to listen to his ravings about assassins, not to clean up after him," McCormick said. "But I suppose, if he was in trouble and there was something I could really do to help—I would."

"When he began to develop this phobia about violence against him, did he ever use a stand-in, a double?"

McCormick nodded, slowly. "It was talked about. In a way it was used. I stood in for him a couple of times—rushed off to an airport in his car, surrounded by his bodyguards, while he went somewhere else. Of course no one close up would mistake me for him; it was just action to distract attention. Reporters, God knows who else, always on his trail."

"The man I saw in Atlantic City on Tuesday, the man in that filthy room, the man guarded by that sharpshooter in a ski mask behind a panel, the man groping for a peanut butter and jelly sandwich, wasn't Barney Steel," Quist said. So the risk was run.

McCormick wasn't moved. "The way he looks now it would be hard to believe he is the much publicized Barney Steel," he said.

"This man had a whole little finger on his right hand," Quist said. "A whole finger with a two inch fingernail to match the others on that hand."

"You're kidding!" McCormick said.

"That's the way it is."

"So there is someone sitting in for him. Long hair? Beard? Old flannel bathrobe and felt slippers?"

"With a whole finger."

"He really has gone off his nut!"

"That's why I took pains to find you, Mike," Quist said. "He was right about me, you know."

"Who was right about you?"

"Barney Steel. I have a curiosity that gets me into trouble. You see, when I was sure that the man who offered me a million dollar job wasn't Barney Steel, then I found myself asking a lot of questions—with no place to ask them. Was this phony Steel interviewing me with Barney Steel's knowledge and consent? That's one question. The next one was, is Barney Steel dead and are Calloway and his other associates trying to keep that a secret so they can hang on to Steel's business empire? And the third question is, is Barney Steel alive, but out of control of his own actions, perhaps gone completely mad and locked up somewhere in a straightjacket? Calloway and the others would still try to hide this in order to maintain control, wouldn't they?"

Mike McCormick sat staring down at the cold coffee in his cup. A nerve began to twitch high up on one cheek. "Interesting possibilities, all of them," he said. He looked at Quist. "Why do you care what the answers are, Mr. Quist? You've been hired to do a profitable job. What difference does it make to you who is actually hiring you?"

Quist shrugged. "I've been asked that question several times in the last twenty-four hours," he said, "by my closest friends. I've thought up a justification, but I have to admit I don't think it's the real answer. I am asked to use my contacts and influence to get three or four hundred important and very rich people to be Steel's guests at the opening of the Steel Palace. If Steel is dead or incompetent, these people will be asked under false pretenses. I will be used to help advance a conspiracy, a fraud. I don't need the money that much, Mike."

"And the real answer?"

"I'm embarrassed to tell you that I'm a little Sir Galahad on a white charger," Quist said. "I don't like powerful men. I probably wouldn't have liked Barney Steel at his best. But I won't sleep well if I ignore a murder or, worse than that, the possibility that a man is a prisoner, a hostage, a victim of his own people."

"So don't take the job," McCormick said.

"It's too late for that, Mike. I can't just walk away, wondering. I may be some kind of a lunatic, but that's the way it is."

"I think I like you for that," McCormick said.

Quist took a long, thin cigar out of the breast pocket of his jacket and lit it. If McCormick was part of any conspiracy against Barney Steel, it was too late to turn back. Two years ago McCormick had walked out on Barney Steel. He couldn't take it any more. An unpleasant thought occurred to Quist. Maybe that was the point when Barney Steel had been murdered or become the captive of his business partners. Maybe McCormick had walked out because there was no longer a Barney Steel to care for! In that case he had been pensioned off, not by Steel but by the conspirators. In that case Quist had delivered himself to the enemy.

"You're asking yourself if I was in on a murder or a conspiracy to hold Barney as a hostage," McCormick said quietly.

"My friend Dan Garvey tells me that someday I'm going to be the victim of my own hunches," Quist said. "Yes, I was wondering if whatever happened to Steel happened two years ago and if you were in on it. But I also had a hunch that you weren't. If that hunch was wrong, you've got me over a barrel, Mike."

McCormick gave him a thin, tired smile. "Whatever the truth is I would of course assure you that your hunch is right. That I'm Barney's friend."

"So I'm stuck with it."

McCormick sat silent for a while and then he seemed to

make up his mind about something.

"There are five men who are basic to Barney Steel Enterprises," he said. "Paul Calloway is a banker and a money genius. He sits on a hundred bank accounts. No one can draw a dime of Steel money without Barney's okay and signature, but Calloway maneuvers millions and millions of dollars. Then there is James Yeager. He oversees all foreign operations. He was an oil man originally. He is a friend of kings, and sheiks, and sultans, and the heads of multinational corporations. He knows more secrets about government manipulations abroad than any man living. His counterpart in the United States is Foster Martin. Martin buys elections all over this country. Bought politicians are what make Barney Steel's business work. Martin also deals with organized crime. He and Yeager and Calloway are the Big Three. Just below them in the power structure is Freddy Lenz. This is a man with a brilliant criminal mind, who thinks up all the sharp deals and crooked corners that have to be negotiated. Then there is Harlan Slade. He is a former marine colonel. He is head of Barney's army, his security force. He is Barney's muscle. He kills for Barney if it's necessary." McCormick drew a deep breath. "Those five men are Barney's strength, but if they were all to turn against him I think not even Barney could stand against them. Surely you couldn't stand against them, Mr. Quist. They could come at you from directions you couldn't imagine."

"What would you do, Mike, if you were in my shoes with my need to know the truth?"

"I would try to be sure that I wasn't dreaming before I made a move. Because without being sure, Mr. Quist, you will be walking into a maze from which there is no escape."

"How do I make sure?"

McCormick stood up and walked over to a window. He stood

there for a moment or two, looking down at the street. Finally he turned back to Quist. "I know how to get to Barney—if he is alive and free. Give me a day or two, Mr. Quist. If I get to him, then you'll know that all you have to do is your job—and mind your own business."

Miss Gloria Chard, the glamorous receptionist in the outer office of Julian Quist Associates, was constantly subjected to male attentions. The mailman delivered wrong letters to the office so that he had occasion to look at Gloria Chard, sitting in the center of her circular desk, smiling at him in a way he didn't quite dare interpret. The boys who delivered luncheon sandwiches to people in the building had a way of appearing before Gloria with orders that belonged somewhere else. Legitimate male clients found themselves reluctant to proceed to inner offices to do their business.

"Gloria," Quist had said of her, "is everybody's whistle stop."

The males in Quist's office, who encountered Gloria every day and who may have dreamed about her, had discovered that despite oozing sex, Gloria was no pushover. Her private life, whatever it was, was carefully guarded. There had been a period when it was assumed that Dan Garvey was the man in her life, but no one was ever able to be quite certain of that.

It was Gloria's habit to make judgments about men. Were they really male, really interested in women? What would they be like out of the business world? Could they be trusted? Could the boss, Julian Quist, trust them? How much was real, and how much was a phony image invented for a purpose? She knew about invented images. That was Quist's business.

The afternoon of the day that Quist went to visit Mike McCormick, a man walked into Gloria Chard's domain who actually jarred her. She was accustomed to movie stars and glamorous public figures. She could look at a Robert Redford or a Warren Beatty, see what it was that set the female population on their ears, and feel nothing in particular. The man who walked in that afternoon was something else. He was, she guessed, in his middle forties which, for him, was obviously the prime of life. He was over six feet tall—as tall as Quist. His hair, a sandy brown, graying slightly at the temples, was crew cut. Man of distinction. His face, his hands, were tanned a mahogany brown. His eyes, a cold gray, surveyed Miss Chard and she was aware, not unhappily, that she was being undressed in public. His body, under a perfectly tailored tropical worsted suit—it was blue-gray, she thought—must be that of an athlete in superb condition. This was about the malest man Gloria had seen in a very long time. To her surprise she felt a little shiver run over her.

"Colonel Harlan Slade to see Mr. Quist," the man said.

"Do you have an appointment, Colonel?"

"Barney Steel Enterprises," the colonel said. That was all the appointment he felt he needed. His voice was clear, cool, not unpleasantly modulated.

"I don't believe Mr. Quist is in," Gloria said. "Let me check."

"He's in," Colonel Slade said.

Gloria picked up the phone that connected her with Connie Parmalee, Quist's secretary. "Colonel Slade of Barney Steel Enterprises to see the boss," Gloria said when Connie picked up. "I've told him Mr. Quist isn't in."

"He just came in the back way," Connie said. "Hold on."

Gloria smiled at Slade and he smiled back. His teeth were very white, very even. Without words he was saying "I told you so."

"The boss will see him," Connie said. "I'll be out."

Gloria looked at the bronzed colonel. "Miss Parmalee will come for you in a moment," she said. "Mr. Quist just came in the back entrance."

"I know," the colonel said. "You are Miss Chard, aren't you?"

Of course there was the nameplate on her desk, but somehow she had the feeling that wasn't where he'd gotten her name. There was something a little eerie about him. He knew that Quist was in. He knew her name.

"Yes, I'm Gloria Chard," she said.

"I expect to be in and out a bit the next two weeks," he said.

He could have said, in so many words, that he would take care of her later. She felt almost relieved when Connie appeared.

"If you'll come this way, Colonel," Connie said.

The cool eyes were fixed on Gloria, as if, she thought, he was memorizing her. He was insufferably self-assured, but that didn't detract from a physical electricity. She wondered if Connie was getting the same charge out of the colonel.

Quist had quite a different reaction to Slade when Connie brought him into the private office. Not so long ago he'd had a rundown on Harlan Slade from Mike McCormick. *"He is Barney's muscle—he kills for Barney if necessary."*

There was nothing of the almost comic rigidity of the military man in Harlan Slade as he faced Quist. This was the perfectly poised, perfectly balanced physical animal, ready to attack or to defend against attack. Quist was reminded of his boyhood and older boys who tried to bully him through their physical superiority. Here it was again. Slade was almost saying *"I can take you with one hand tied behind me."*

Quist remained seated at his chromium-trimmed desk. He

made no move to shake hands with his visitor. He anticipated a bone crusher which always annoyed him. "Sit down, Colonel. Can I offer you a cigar, cigarette? If you care for a drink, do help yourself at the bar in the corner there."

"I suspect you know who I am, Mr. Quist."

"Oh, yes. Head of Barney Steel's security force."

"You've been busy catching up on us," Slade said, smiling his white smile.

"I like to know as much as possible about the people who are using my services," Quist said. "I suspect you're highly efficient at your job."

The white smile widened. The colonel seemed to be balanced on the balls of his feet, ready to deliever a counter-punch. "Let's see how good I am," he said. "You breakfasted in your apartment on Beekman Place with Miss Morton, the lady who lives with you. After that you visited a lieutenant of Homicide at police headquarters downtown. From there you went to Sutton Place where you spent an hour with Mike McCormick, a former employee of Mr. Steel's. You came back here and used a service elevator at the rear of the building to come up to your office. Efficient enough, Mr. Quist?"

Quist's face had turned rock hard. He stood up. "Let's consider this interview at an end, Colonel," he said.

The colonel's smile turned mocking. "Did I slip up somewhere?" he asked.

"Like most people of your mentality you slipped up on an essential fact," Quist said. "You are so proud of your skills at surveillance that you didn't take the trouble to make any assessment of the person you set yourself to watch. I wouldn't work for five minutes for an employer who had me followed, watched, would probably read my mail, bug my telephone."

"Mr. Steel would not hire anyone without finding out all

there is to know about him. In his world it isn't safe not to know everything about anyone who is going to work for him, spend time under the same roof with him. Because, of course, you will be spending time at the Steel Palace in the near future."

"I don't think I will be spending time at the Palace," Quist said. "I know damn well I won't be working for the man who hired me day before yesterday."

"Just because he had you followed?" Slade asked. He was still smiling. "You'd throw away a million dollars just for that?"

"You go back to the Steel Palace, Colonel, and tell your people I'm not interested in their job or their money unless the game is played by my rules. And the first rule is that you and your trailers stay off my back. I'll only reconsider when I'm assured of that."

The colonel, it appeared, was not a blusterer. "I think you've guessed wrong about me, Mr. Quist," he said. "I wasn't trying to show you how clever I am by running down your day's doings. I wanted you to know how efficient we are, not to threaten you, but to show you how important we can be to you. You're going to need me and my people."

"For what?"

"We are living in violent times, Quist. I assume you and your staff are already compiling a list of guests to invite to the grand opening. That list will be composed of the richest and most important men in the world. People like that, Mr. Quist, are the targets for all the crackpots, the dissenters, the revolutionaries, the communists. They daren't travel for fear of hijackers. They are like Barney, they have to stay inside their own fortresses, inside their own walls, inside their own borders. The only way they will be persuaded to cross oceans and come into a strange land is to be assured, beyond question, that an impenetrable security will surround them, coming and going. Barney expects me to provide that security. It will obviously be your job to convince our potential guests that it will be completely safe for them to come to the Steel Palace. I came here to outline our security plans to you so you can pass it on to the potential guests. I chose the wrong method of giving you a sample of our effectiveness. I apologize. As for getting off your back—may I say I don't think I need to know any more about you than I already know. Perhaps we can achieve some kind of mutual respect for each other in the future."

A light blinked on the phone at Quist's elbow. He picked up the receiver.

"Yes?"

"Eric Tranter here to see you," Connie told him. "Shall I ask him to wait?"

"Bring him in, Connie," Quist said. He put down the phone and leaned back in his chair. He seemed to relax. "In connection with that guest list, Colonel, I'd asked a friend of mine to drop by to give me advice. He's a State Department man named Eric Tranter. Perhaps you've heard of him?"

Slade's tight, white smile never deserted him. "Would you believe I have an appointment with him for later this afternoon?"

"So, two birds with one stone," Quist said.

Eric Tranter's large, gold-rimmed glasses gave him the look of a college professor. His summer-tweed jacket had suede patches at the elbows. His gray slacks and button-down white shirt completed what had been a sort of campus uniform a generation back. He was slim, his movements slightly awkward, his smile boyish and deprecating. You got the impression, however, that whatever his expertise was, he was first class at it. He was Quist's age, just shy of forty, and he and Quist had been friends since their college days.

"A handy coincidence, Colonel," Tranter said when Quist introduced them. "I suspect the business you had in mind for later is also Julian's business."

"An offshoot of it, at least," Slade said.

Tranter sat down in one of the chrome-trimmed armchairs, and stretched long legs out in front of him. He began to fill a pipe from an oilskin pouch, completing the picture of yesterday's campus. "Barney Steel's guest list is, I suppose, the first order of business," he said.

"The guest list is Quist's business," Slade said. "Getting those people here and back again in safety is mine. I've been explaining to Quist that unless the potential guests can be guaranteed complete security they aren't going to accept Barney's invitation."

"That may be open to debate," Tranter said. He held a lighter to his pipe and puffed out a cloud of smoke. " 'Invitation' is a polite word for summons, wouldn't you say, Colonel? The kind of people on the list can't refuse a summons from Barney Steel. They'll be happy with your assurances of security, but they'll come with or without it. Turn down Barney Steel Enterprises and you run the risk of painful reprisals. Right, Colonel?"

Slade's smile widened. "I suppose you could say that."

"Isn't that stretching Steel's power a little far?" Quist asked. "We're talking about rulers, dictators, oil controllers, the heads of multinational corporations. Surely Barney Steel can't just beckon such men."

"I think even the President of the United States might hesitate to turn down an 'invitation' from Barney Steel," Tranter said. "At least until it was quite certain he wasn't going to run for another term. I don't suppose too many people would believe that Barney Steel could swing an election in this country, but I have to tell you I believe he could."

Quist's eyes narrowed. He was thinking of the man in the soiled bathrobe and pajamas, the man with the long hair and beard and grimy fingernails, he'd seen at the Steel Palace. A stand-in, Quist was convinced, but he wouldn't have appeared as he did unless that was the way the real Barney Steel looked today. If the real Barney Steel was alive . . .

"We can offer our own jet planes," Slade said, "manned by our own pilots, protected by our own security guards, at the airports, in flight. We can, in fact, surround and protect them from their own front doors into the Palace, and every step they take while they are there. The security measures we have set up to protect Barney will make his guests just as untouchable as he is."

"As I understand it you are inviting six hundred name guests, along with their wives, their official entourages," Tranter said. "That has to be something like two thousand people."

"The Palace can accommodate twenty-two hundred and forty guests," Slade said.

"And you can provide each one of them with one or more guards?"

"Let's just say that I command a substantial army," Slade said. "Our guests will be safer than they are in their own homes."

"And if they want to bring their own trusted bodyguards?"

"The only people I trust are my people," Slade said. "Anyone involved with security will be under my orders. No one will carry any kind of a weapon except my people."

"Pretty hard to enforce that, I should think," Tranter said.

"There are electronic detection systems all over the Palace," Slade said. "No one can board one of our planes without passing the same kind of electronic eye. We can enforce it."

Tranter put down his pipe which he didn't seem to be able to get going properly. "With such an efficient setup, what was it you wanted to talk to me about, Colonel?" he asked.

Slade's smile faded, and the cool eyes fixed on Tranter. "Many of the invited people are of some consequence to the State Department," he said. "I wanted to make it absolutely clear to you that they will be safe, that we can guarantee the security."

"So let's say that you've convinced me," Tranter said. "For the sake of argument."

"I don't want any bungling assistance from the FBI or the CIA or the Secret Service," Slade said. "I want that word passed on by your department, Mr. Tranter. I want it clearly understood."

"You sound, Colonel, as though you are giving orders to the United States government," Tranter said.

"You could say that," Slade said blandly. "I am prepared to keep government agencies informed of every step we take, the guest lists, the men under my command. But I will not have any contradictory plans, duplication of assignments, orders coming from somebody else."

"And if the government doesn't agree to this?"

"I'll have to tell Barney that the government is obstructing his wishes," Slade said.

"And God will speak?" Quist asked, not believing what he was hearing.

"I want hourly, even minute by minute reports from you, Mr Quist, on the names you come up with for invitation. Barney will approve or disapprove them. We have very little time to prepare for several hundred guests to be properly guarded. I think that's all, gentlemen."

Quist had pressed a button under the edge of his desk, and

Connie appeared in the doorway to her private office. There was a curious sphinx-like look in the eyes behind the tinted granny-glasses. The intercom had been open between her office and Quist's and she had been able to hear the entire exchange.

"Will you show Colonel Slade out, please, Connie," Quist said.

Slade was apparently not quite ready to go. "I was asked to tell you, Quist, that Barney expects you and Miss Morton to take up residence at the Palace no later than a week from now. It is, as you are aware, impossible for him to work with you at this distance. You may bring any other members of your staff you choose. Just let Paul Calloway know when you are coming and how many people you are bringing."

"Or whether I decide not to come at all," Quist said. "So much power, Colonel, has the unfortunate effect of making me want to throw up."

Slade's white smile reappeared. "With a million bucks dangling in front of you? I think you'll learn to live with it." He turned to Tranter. "There's no need our keeping our later appointment, Mr. Tranter. I've said all I meant to say to you then. You will, I trust, let me know if there is any question about the plan of operation I've outlined."

"And if there is you will speak to someone more important than I am?" Tranter said.

"Barney will speak to someone more important than you, Mr. Tranter," Slade said. "Good afternoon, gentlemen."

The colonel followed Connie out of the office. Tranter picked up his pipe and concentrated on getting it going again.

"I'll be a sonofabitch!" Quist said

Tranter smiled like a man hiding pain. "Not many people get a chance to see who calls the turns in this cockeyed world," he said.

"It's out of some dime-novel melodrama," Quist said. "Can they really tell you where to head in, Eric?"

"I am just a messenger boy," Tranter said. "I think the powers-that-be will arrange to accommodate Barney Steel."

"If Barney Steel exists," Quist said.

Tranter looked up, startled. "Just what the hell does that mean, Julian?"

Quist told him briefly what he suspected, what he guessed might be the truth. Tranter listened, pipe gone out again. He was a man accustomed to hearing about elaborate political conspiracies. When Quist had finished he sat silent for a moment or two, staring down at the toes of his neatly polished shoes.

"I buy the idea that an attempt was made to flimflam you with a stand-in," he said, finally. "I don't buy the idea that Barney Steel is dead. A hostage, held by his own people?" He shrugged. "Farfetched but possible."

"I may have a believable answer in a day or two," Quist said, and he told Tranter about his visit with Mike McCormick. "Why do you write off the idea that Steel is dead?"

"Because too many people would be rushing to grab off a piece of the cake," Tranter said. "The cake being Barney Steel's world. Each subdivision of that empire, Julian, would be a world in itself. Most men would be satisfied with a piece of it and the men close to Barney Steel would each be after his share. The repercussions would be as detectable by our government as an earthquake. There hasn't been a hint of any such upheaval."

Quist got up and moved restlessly away from his desk and across the office to the completely appointed bar in the corner. "Yardarm or no yardarm," he said, as he poured himself a Jack Daniels on the rocks with a splash of water. "Join me, Eric?"

"A smallish scotch," Tranter said.

Quist crossed back with a drink for his friend. "There's been a great deal in print lately about the overblown power of the big multinational corporations," he said, headed back for his desk. "But hundreds of them, Eric! And here I get a picture of Barney Steel telling them all how to function, all where to head in. I don't find it believable."

"Words make it sound too simple," Tranter said. "Barney Steel isn't some tinhorn fascist dictator issuing orders and making speeches from a balcony. You've seen the commander of his army, but that army doesn't seize territory. It's a police force. It protects his person, his people, his property."

"Steel rules the world with money," Quist said.

"Money is just pieces of gold, or silver, or copper, or paper," Tranter said. "Economics One, my friend. Your money is what you get in exchange for labor. That labor is what's valuable, the work done, not the paper you deposit in the bank or carry around in your pocket. What Steel owns is what counts, and it's complex. Oil, steel, airlines, railroads, hotels, television and radio networks. He's acquired these things, piece by piece, over a lifetime of brilliant business maneuvers. His control comes, not from offering money and bribes, but from withholding what he owns from people who need what he's got. He has enough to manage the whole world economy."

"It's hard to take in."

"He's a very modern pirate," Tranter said. "He differs from the old-timers, the Morgans, the Rockefellers, the Carnegies. They were public personalities—J. P. Morgan and his nose, John D. Rockefeller and his ten-cent tips, Carnegie and his public charities. Barney Steel, after an early flamboyance with glamorous ladies, slipped out of view. He could walk down Fifth Avenue and nobody would recognize him. Privacy and secrecy became the keys to his operation. He has never been a

Bismarck or a Hitler or a Mussolini or a Churchill. He operates unseen and almost unknown. That's why he can get away with using a stand-in or a double. Only a smart alec like you would notice the presence of a little finger that shouldn't be there. But the power is there and he knows better than anyone how to use it. You'll have no trouble, Julian, filling his Palace with guests. Even on such short notice. They'll come, not because they will enjoy his luxurious hospitality, not because they like to gamble, but because it is too dangerous to say no to him. If anyone does say no, you can be certain you've selected an unimportant candidate. If you can't be hurt by Barney Steel, you are distinctly small fry."

"You understand what's bothering me?" Quist asked. "It's hard to live with unanswered questions."

"It can be nothing, Julian," Tranter said. "They'll pay you a million dollars, which is a huge fee. But you're just running a party for them. You insisted on seeing Steel, they wanted your skills, so they pretended to agree and fed you to a stand-in. There's nothing sinister about that. You may be annoyed that they pulled a fast one on you, but it doesn't follow that there's some kind of sinister plot in the works. If Barney Steel was dead, I can almost guarantee we'd have felt the earth shake a little in Washington. Let me say, it seems to me you could go to your man Calloway and tell him you want to see the real Barney Steel, the one with only half a finger. He'll probably laugh and tell you Steel is a very busy man and they thought they could satisfy you with a stand-in."

"And take me to the real Steel?"

"Why not?"

"Because the real Steel is dead or locked up in a padded cell somewhere."

Tranter sighed. "You're really bitten by this bug, aren't you?"

"Seems like."

"So you wait till your man McCormick reports back and you know something for real. Meanwhile you just go about your job of collecting high-powered guests for the party."

"You could be right," Quist said.

Yet every instinct he had for danger warned him.

The real reason for Eric Tranter's visit to Julian Quist Associates had nothing to do with Quist's suspicions. The meeting with Colonel Harlan Slade had been accidental. Tranter had come with an attaché case filled with lists of names, a sort of State Department's Who's Who of the richest, most important, most influential men in existence.

Quist had brought back from Atlantic City the three hundred names already invited by Barney Steel Enterprises. Every one of those names was to be found on Tranter's lists.

"I would have marked every one of them as my first choices," Tranter said. "Barney Steel doesn't miss a trick."

"Somebody doesn't miss a trick," Quist said.

"Oh, brother, you've really got it," Tranter said.

He and Quist worked far into the night, interrupted only by a supper brought in by Connie Parmalee. Quist had anticipated it would take days and days to come up with another three to four hundred names. By two o'clock in the morning, thanks to Tranter's knowledge, they had compiled a list of four hundred and fifty names. They needed only three hundred acceptances from that group to fill the Steel Palace for its opening.

Quist went over to the bar and poured two stiff nightcaps.

Every muscle in his body ached. "I feel as if I'd been carrying bricks," he said.

"The Steel Palace people should be very pleased with the results," Tranter said. He stood up and stretched wearily. "You owe me one, Julian. You could have spent a lifetime at this without my lists."

"Name it," Quist said, bringing his friend a stiff scotch-on-the-rocks.

"Six hundred of the richest and most powerful men in the world will have accepted Steel's invitations by tomorrow at this time," Tranter said. He sipped his drink gratefully. "They will have accepted because it would be unwise for them to refuse. In addition to those six hundred men there is your partner Dan Garvey, your friend Lieutenant Kreevich and me—six hundred and three people who would advise you, if asked, to forget about your suspicions. Whatever is going on in Barney Steel Enterprises is not your business, and neither you nor any other one man has what it takes to stop whatever it is. You have nothing at stake. Let the man-eating tigers destroy each other, if that's what the game is. Collect your fee. Limit your chance-taking to the roulette wheels, or the blackjack tables, or the dice games. All you can lose that way is money."

Quist nodded but he didn't answer. Tranter knew his man. Reason was not something to which Quist was prepared to listen just now. Perhaps tomorrow the facts of life would sink in. Tranter hoped so. He knew that to argue now would only serve to reinforce Quist's stubbornness.

The two men parted on the sidewalk outside the office building. Tranter took the first taxi that came along. Normally, Quist walked the ten blocks to his apartment, but tonight he waited for a second cab. He couldn't remember being so tired.

He let himself into his Beekman Place duplex a few minutes

before three. A lamp burned on the center table in the living room, a piece of paper propped up against it. He tossed his briefcase on the couch and picked up the paper.

"You dirty stay-out!" was written on it in Lydia's neat script.

He glanced up the winding stair to the second floor. She would be there, waiting for him. She needed her sleep like a child. Perhaps, he thought, that was why she stayed so lovely, so fresh.

He turned out lights and went up. From the doorway of his dressing room he looked into the bedroom. She was there, in their king-sized bed, her dark hair spread out on the pillow, one arm thrown up over her head.

Quist showered. He felt grimy after the night's work. Then he slipped into bed beside Lydia. She made some half-asleep love sounds and her arm came down and went around him. There were times for passionate lovemaking and times just to love. They both felt safe and secure and wanted, just lying together, touching.

But sound sleep didn't come for Quist in spite of his fatigue. He dozed off and then came wide awake, retreating from some instantly forgotten nightmarish fantasy. He came out of one of those doze-offs, aware that the little red light was blinking on the bedside phone. Gently, he moved Lydia's arm, turned on his side, and picked up the phone.

"Yes?"

"Julian? Mark Kreevich here." The homicide man's voice sounded cold and distant.

"What's up?" Quist asked.

"Michael McCormick," Kreevich said.

"What about him?" Quist asked. He felt his hand tighten on the phone.

"Shot and beaten to death in the men's room at the airport

in Atlantic City," Kreevich said. "The local homicide boys identified him, called here since a Master Charge card they found on him indicated that he lived here in New York. No arrest. No leads, they say. They assume it was a mugging, probably by some sexual pervert since he wasn't robbed. Are you there, Julian?"

"Yes." Quist could feel the pulse beating at his temple.

"You knew McCormick was going to Atlantic City?"

"Yes."

"So stay out of it, friend. Let the cops handle it."

"Thanks for calling," Quist said, and put down the phone.

Lydia was sitting up in bed, a sheet pulled around her. Quist told her the news. He got out of bed, headed for the dressing room. Lydia followed him in a moment, having put on a robe. He was already dressing.

"Where are you going, Julian?" she asked.

"Those bastards killed him!" Quist said. He couldn't shake the smiling image of Colonel Harlan Slade. He could hear Mike McCormick's voice. *"He is Barney's muscle. He kills for Barney if it's necessary."*

"It's not your job, Julian. It's not your responsibility," Lydia said.

He turned and faced her, his eyes so cold they frightened her. "I sent him there," he said. "I *am* responsible, and by God—"

She reached him, her hands raised to his face. "Please, Julian—"

"See if you can get me a seat on the next flight to Atlantic City," he said.

Part II

1

In the plane, on the way to Atlantic City, Quist's first surge of anger began to subside, to be replaced by an attempt at a reasonable analysis of the situation. He was no less determined to get at the truth, to square accounts for Mike McCormick, but he was reminded of an old caution he'd had from Mark Kreevich in past situations. The homicide man was fond of saying, "Don't bull-in-a-china-shop it."

One thing was certain. His hunch about Mike McCormick had proved out, tragically, violently, but proved out. Mike had gone after the truth about what was going on in the Steel Palace and he must have found it. Looking out the plane window at the first signs of dawn, Quist wondered, with a bitter taste in his mouth, why Mike hadn't telephoned. He had given Mike his private numbers. The little man who had devoted his life to Barney Steel wouldn't have risked using a phone in the Steel Palace if he had been there. Phones there would almost certainly have been monitored. Mike must have headed for the airport for the return journey, planning to use a pay phone there, and been stopped, wiped out, before he could use it. Or had he been so sure he wasn't detected that he hadn't considered a phone call in the early hours of the morning dangerous?

Quist found himself looking over the passengers on his plane.

There were less than a dozen people, only one of them a woman. An elderly woman immersed in a paperback novel. Harlan Slade had covered every move he'd made yesterday. Was one of the sleepy-looking passengers a Slade man? He had the uncomfortable feeling that he was now being permanently watched. There need not be anyone on the plane, of course. The first stop on this flight was Atlantic City. A phone call from a trailer in New York would have someone waiting for him at the airport in Atlantic City.

There was the smell of ocean salt in the air when Quist disembarked. The sun was up now, and it was going to be a hazy, hot summer day. No one appeared to be waiting for him. The elderly woman was met by another elderly woman. Only two other passengers got off. Eight or ten people got on. There was little or no passenger traffic in the terminal. Quist looked for the men's room, saw the sign, and headed for it. He was stopped before he reached the door by two plainclothes cops who showed their badges. The men's room, he was told, was off limits at the moment.

"I know that someone was killed in there early this morning," Quist said. "He was someone I knew. I'd like to talk to the man in charge."

The man in charge, summoned by one of the plainclothes officers, introduced himself as Sergeant Luke Tabor. He was a big man who looked as though he'd slept in his clothes. He needed a shave. His sleepy eyes were deceptive.

"What can I do for you, Mr. Quist?" he asked, after Quist had identified himself.

"Mike McCormick was an acquaintance of mine," Quist said.

"You heard what happened to him on the radio?"

Quist shook his head "Lieutenant Kreevich, Manhattan

Homicide, is also a friend of mine. He called me to tell me about McCormick after he'd been asked questions by your department."

"By me," Tabor said. "And you came hotfooting it down here? Why, Mr. Quist?"

"I have other business down here," Quist said.

"What business?"

"I'm a public relations man working for Barney Steel."

Tabor's sleepy eyes narrowed. "You knew McCormick when he was working for Steel?"

"No. I've only been on Steel's payroll for three days, four counting today," Quist said. "I met McCormick for the first time day before yesterday."

"Then you can't be of very much help to us, can you?" Tabor said. "Except for one thing."

"And that is?"

"We don't know whether McCormick was just arriving in Atlantic City or just leaving. When we identified him we made inquiries at the hotel—the Steel Palace. No one there had seen him. He wasn't expected. They can't account for his being here."

"I think he was leaving," Quist said. "I think he came down here yesterday."

"But you don't know for certain?"

"No."

Tabor fished a cigarette out of his pocket and lit it with a cheap lighter. "The woods are full of freaks and crazies," he said. "McCormick was killed about two in the morning. There would have been a plane for New York in about a half an hour. A passenger, waiting for that plane, found him when he went in there to relieve himself. Lying in his own blood, two shots in the back of his head. Then whoever it was made sure by clubbing him with the proverbial blunt instrument. No gun, no club."

"Is there a phone in there?" Quist asked.

"Matter of fact there is," Tabor said. "He was standing right by the booth when he was shot."

Quist felt his jaw muscles tighten. A few minutes more and Mike McCormick might have gotten to him with facts. "Who did you talk to at the Steel Palace?" he asked.

"Their security chief."

"Colonel Slade?"

"His name is Slade, I don't know about the 'Colonel'."

"Kreevich told me you thought the killer was some kind of sex pervert. Why?"

Tabor shrugged. "He wasn't robbed. He had over a hundred dollars in cash on him. In the middle of the night some of these sex nuts hang around. He probably made some kind of a pass at McCormick, and when McCormick tried to shove him off, he let him have it. There's no accounting for that kind of character."

"You don't think somebody was after McCormick, followed him here and hit him? It could have been some kind of a contract, couldn't it?"

"Could be," Tabor said. "We don't have any leads. You have any reason to think there could have been a contract out on him?"

"McCormick was a close friend of Barney Steel's," Quist said. "Grew up with him, worked for him all his life until two years ago, when he retired."

"Yeah. Slade told me he retired two years ago," Tabor said. "Had no reason connected with Steel for being in Atlantic City."

"Even Colonel Slade can't know that for sure," Quist said.

He was working around to something that could help. "McCormick knew things about Steel, personal things, private things, that nobody else knows. He knew the whole of Steel's past until two years ago. Something out of that past could be threatening Steel, and McCormick came down here to warn him. That's a guess, of course. The security is so tight around Steel that even an old friend couldn't get to him. Before he could find a way to get to Steel someone out of the past got to McCormick and wiped him out. In that sense it could be a contract."

The ash dribbled off Tabor's cigarette and down his shirt front. "How good a guess is it, Mr. Quist? Did McCormick tell you something when you met him—day before yesterday, was it?"

"We talked, very casually, about how many enemies Steel had made over the years," Quist said. "A man with Steel's wealth and power always has enemies."

"But you didn't talk about anyone in particular?"

"We talked about the fact that Steel is terrified someone will get to him. He lives in a boarded-up room at the top of the hotel, surrounded by armed men. That's how scared he is. When I tried to see him they pulled a fast one on me. They ran in a double on me. If I were you, Sergeant—if I were handling this case—I'd go talk to Barney Steel. He may not even know what's happened to McCormick. On the other hand, McCormick may have gotten to Steel without Colonel Slade knowing it. If he did, Steel could give you a lead to the killer."

"It's worth a try," Tabor said. He dropped his cigarette on the tile floor and stepped on it.

"Just so they don't pull the same fast one on you they did on me," Quist said, "I'll give you a tip, Sergeant. The little finger on the right hand of the real Barney Steel is missing at the middle joint. If the Steel you see has a whole finger, you'll know they've rung in the double on you."

"You're full of interesting tidbits," Tabor said.

"I admit I was annoyed when they tried to pass off the stand-in on me," Quist said "You could say they gave me the finger."

Tabor wasn't amused. "You headed for the Steel Palace now?" he asked.

"Yes."

"If you come across anything interesting give me a call," Tabor said.

Shortly before eight o'clock a taxi drove Quist to the porticoed entrance to the Steel Palace. Although the Palace wasn't open for business a uniformed doorman opened the taxi door and told Quist, courteously, that the hotel wasn't open—unless he had business with the management. Quist gave his name and the doorman gave him a polite salute and stood aside, holding the cab door open. He didn't consult a list. It was as though he expected this particular visitor.

"I'm looking for Mr. Calloway," Quist said.

"Across the lobby to your left when you go through the front door, sir."

There was a strange atmosphere inside the Palace. No guests, but there were three clerks at the registration desk, uniformed bellboys in position. "A dry run," Calloway had called it. Later on Quist was to learn that clean-up crews went to work at five in the morning, the kitchens were in operation to feed the large staff. Calloway and other members of the top echelon of Steel's empire had already moved into suites and were being served as the glamorous guests would be served later. By opening day there wouldn't be a single hitch in what was planned to be Swiss-watch perfection.

Calloway was seated at his desk in the office Quist had visited before. He looked up over his reading glasses at Quist with a faintly amused smile.

"We were expecting you, Mr. Quist," he said.

"I find that interesting," Quist said, "since I hadn't planned to come until the early hours this morning."

"We've had a man at the airport since we got the news about poor Mike McCormick," Calloway said. "He saw you arrive and talk to the police there."

Slade efficiency, Quist thought.

Calloway took off his glasses and put them down on the desk. "We are, of course, concerned here, and Barney is deeply distressed. Mike was very close to him over the years." He drew a deep breath. "I guess we owe you some kind of apology."

"For what?" Quist asked.

"Trying to pass off Drysdale on you as Barney the other day."

"Drysdale?"

"Fred Drysdale is an actor who fronts for Barney from time to time. We wanted your services and Barney simply won't see strangers. How did Fred trip up with you?"

"The little finger on his right hand," Quist said. "Otherwise his performance was perfect." He hesitated. "You know from Slade that I went to see McCormick in New York. I feel responsible for what's happened to him."

"Why? Who could foresee some sexual creep would attack him at the airport?"

"If that's what happened to him," Quist said quietly.

Calloway kept his eyes averted, twisting and turning a small brass ashtray on the desk. "We live in times of terror," he said. "That's why the guests who come to our opening must be so carefully guarded. Mike was a nice, innocuous little man, but he wasn't safe. It could happen to any of us."

"He came here to see Barney Steel," Quist said.

Calloway looked up, his boyish face a mask of innocence. "Tragically, he never got here," he said. "Barney would have seen him, of course. There was no favor that Mike could have asked that Barney wouldn't have granted."

"Mike came here to make sure Barney Steel is alive," Quist said.

Calloway indulged in a small chuckle. "Dear me, Mr. Quist, your imagination must have run riot after you saw through Drysdale's little impersonation. But I assure you, Mike never got here. I assume he was waylaid at the airport before he could get a taxi to bring him out here."

It was a bland performance, Quist thought. "I suppose there's no reason why my doubts can't be put to rest," he said.

"By seeing Barney—the real Barney? Of course. He's been alerted that you're here and what your concerns must have been. You can go up to him now, if you like."

"I would like," Quist said. He opened a briefcase he was holding in his lap. "I have a list of names I compiled for you last night."

"Splendid," Calloway said, taking the sheaf of papers from Quist. "Jim Yeager and I will look it over while you're with Barney and we can discuss it later." He looked past Quist who was suddenly aware that the man with the shoulder holster who had ridden up and down in the elevator on his first visit had come silently into the office behind him. "Mulloy will take you up to Barney's room. May I remind you, Mr. Quist, if you are carrying a gun it will be detected and I can't answer for the consequences."

He got up from his desk and walked to the office door with Quist. At that moment a curious parade was taking place from the elevators toward the main dining room. At the center of it was an enormous black man wearing what looked like a British army uniform, weighted down with medals. An officer's cap was set at a jaunty angle on his head and he was carrying a swagger stick. He must, Quist thought, weigh over three hundred pounds and yet he moved with a kind of youthful quickness and agility. He was surrounded by a bevy of laughing girls, all smartly dressed, some black, some white. The big man's laughter at a joke boomed out like cheerful thunder. Then he spotted Calloway, Quist, and the bodyguard standing in the office doorway. His smile was dazzling as he raised his right hand in a crisp, military salute.

"Good morning, Mr. Calloway—gentlemen. A magnificent morning, I call it."

"Good morning, Your Excellency," Calloway said.

The black man spoke an impeccable Oxford English. "I am taking my ladies for what I hope will be a typical American breakfast." He made an all-embracing gesture toward the girls. "Waiting for them to pretty themselves has me on the verge of starvation."

The parade moved on and disappeared into the dining area.

"Who on earth?" Quist asked.

"He is the president of one of the newly emerging African nations," Calloway said. "I find myself confused by the new countries. Could it be Kambashi? His name is Lamu Sharah. The ladies are, in polite language, his wives."

"Brother!" Quist said. He remembered the name. It was on the list given him by Calloway on his first visit. Sharah had also been on Eric Tranter's list.

"A cheerful tyrant and bully," Tranter had said.

"He was here on a diplomatic mission to Washington," Calloway said. "It seemed complicated for him to return home and come back again for the grand opening, so Barney arranged for him and his entourage to be our first guests. The opening is only twelve days away. His idea of a typical American breakfast is a four-rib roast of beef with side dishes! When he has digested that, he will spend two hours in the Palace's gymnasium—workout, sauna bath, the complete treatment. In the afternoon he will entertain himself with his 'wives.' At five o'clock a case of iced champagne will be delivered to his suite which will be consumed in an hour or so. Then they all go to an elaborate seven-course dinner." Calloway smiled. "He skips a midday meal. Has to watch his weight, he says. After dinner they proceed to the gambling rooms where all of them lose enough money to more than pay for the day's free entertainment. That is, you might say, the principle on which the Steel Palace operates. Our dealers and croupiers are getting plenty of practice for the big moment."

"Where does his money come from?" Quist asked.

Calloway shrugged. "Oil, copper, diamonds. Would you like to go on up to Barney now, Mr. Quist?"

It was all working with deceptive smoothness. The man with the machine pistol waited by the elevators. Mulloy, the man with the bulging shoulder holster, boarded the private lift with Quist and rode to the roof area. Mulloy was not a conversationalist. He gestured toward the passage where Quist knew he would have to pass the inspection of the electronic eye. The door beyond this opened automatically as before and Quist went into the cluttered, stiflingly hot room.

Someone sat in the Morris chair looking exactly like the man Quist had seen on his first visit, straggling gray hair down over the glittering black eyes, the soiled bathrobe and pajamas, the felt bedroom slippers. The only difference in the room this time was that the wall behind the chair was lighted and the man with the ski mask and the high-powered rifle with the telescopic sight was visible and ready. As Quist approached, the man in the Morris chair raised his right hand in a halting gesture. The grimy, long fingernails, like claws, were there—except on the little finger which was amputated at the middle joint.

"That is far enough, Mr. Quist."

The voice was different, deeper and a little stronger than the stand-in's voice had been.

"I regret that this visit is necessary," Barney Steel said. It had to be Barney Steel, didn't it?

"I imagined all kinds of disasters had overtaken you, Mr. Steel," Quist said.

"I know. And most unfortunate for Mike McCormick. You convinced him there might be something to your imaginings."

"I'm afraid I did," Quist said. He found his eyes straying toward the man with the rifle. He saw now that it wasn't glass that separated the man from the room but some kind of theatrical scrim or netting.

"Mike was a loyal friend," Steel said. "He came here to help and it cost him his life. Perhaps it will help you to understand why I stay hidden here in this room, protected by my guards. There is no other safe place for me or my associates."

"The police believe that McCormick was done in by some kind of sex pervert," Quist said.

"I know what the police believe, Mr. Quist."

"Don't you believe it?" Quist asked.

The long fingernails scratched at the board across the arms of the Morris chair—just as the stand-in's fingernails had scratched at it. "When anything happens to anyone remotely connected with me, Mr. Quist, I find myself wondering about the coincidence. The fact is that Mike never got to see me. He would, of course, have been received and reassured that your imaginings had no substance."

The bright black eyes peering at Quist through the scraggly hair had a hypnotic quality to them that the stand-in's had not. You could believe that this was a man, despite the rest of his appearance and his surroundings, who ruled an empire.

"It was a miscalculation," Steel said.

"What was a miscalculation, Mr. Steel?"

"Trying to pass off Drysdale on you," Steel said. "I don't like to see strangers, Mr. Quist. I don't even like to see friends. I am not proud of what has—has happened to me, physically. There seemed to be no reason to suppose you wouldn't accept Drysdale as me. We wanted your help. There was nothing to agree on except the price. Drysdale knew exactly what to offer you. It should have worked perfectly smoothly with no harm to you. The business aspects of it were quite straightforward. But you noticed—" And Steel held up his mutilated finger.

"Diana Lewis told me you got that in an air battle in Korea," Quist said.

"How is Diana?" Steel asked.

"She's well. A great success. She wishes she could see you."

A slight shudder moved the shriveled body in the bathrobe. "It must be obvious to you how impossible that is," Steel said. For the first time he turned his head to glance at the man with the rifle. "There are dangerous consequences to what has happened, Mr. Quist."

"In what way dangerous?"

"You have talked to a great many people about your not unkind concern for me. A policeman in New York, a man from the State Department, Diana, Mike, your staff almost certainly. It is a rumor that could spread like a forest fire."

"But since I now know there was no basis for my concerns—?"

"Can you stop the fire, Mr. Quist? We will know when the stock market opens this morning—or tomorrow morning. If I were to be rumored dead and certain investors were to believe the rumor, there would be a panic in the money markets all over the world—New York, London, Paris, Tokyo. It could strike a crippling blow to many of my enterprises. Many of the people invited to the opening of this establishment would have second thoughts. Millions of dollars invested here would be endangered."

"It should be simple enough to put an end to rumors," Quist said.

"How, Mr. Quist?"

"Call a press conference—to show the news people what is being planned here at the Palace. Make a public appearance at that time. End of gossip."

"Impossible!" Steel almost shouted.

"A barber, a bath, and some fresh clothes," Quist suggested. He wiped at his face with his handkerchief. The heat in the room seemed suddenly intolerable.

"Nothing would hide what has happened to me physically," Steel said. His voice shook. "This—this rotting away would produce the same kind of panic in the money markets. My death or the imminent likelihood of my death would have the same results. No, Mr. Quist, I think we have to go about it in another fashion."

"I take it you have another idea."

Steel was silent for a moment, clawing at the board in front of him. "I think we have to enlarge the scope of your job for us," he said.

"Enlarge how?"

"Calloway and Yeager and Colonel Slade are prepared to discuss it with you," Steel said. "We have to take extraordinary measures, Mr. Quist. I trust you will not be too inconvenienced."

"I think you'd better explain," Quist said. He felt his muscles tensing. He was aware that he was being threatened in some fashion.

Steel leaned back in his chair and the bright eyes were suddenly closed. "I—I am too tired to discuss it with you," he said "I'm sorry for what has happened. I appreciate your decent concerns which have brought it about. But we have no choice but to find a way out of the dilemma in which you've placed us."

"Now look here, Mr. Steel—"

The claw-like hand silenced him. Someone touched Quist on the shoulder and he spun around. Mulloy, the bodyguard, had come up behind him without a sound.

"Mr. Calloway is waiting for you downstairs," Mulloy said.

Barney Steel opened his eyes. "I won't see you again, Mr Quist," he said "I wish we could have met under happier circumstances."

That, apparently, was that.

Stepping off the elevator in the lobby, Quist felt the same relief at escaping from the hothouse of a room as on his first visit. The bright sun, the cool breeze off the ocean, made it seem as if he were emerging into a new world. He blotted at the perspiration that still dampened his forehead. From some distance away he heard the joyous, thunderous laughter of Lamu Sharah, the man with many wives.

"Into the office please, Mr. Quist," Mulloy said.

Quist had an impulse to walk out the front door onto the public street and to hell with them. Yet he knew, somehow, that he wouldn't be allowed to make it if he tried. The bright lobby with its glittering glass chandeliers and its magnificent paintings seemed to have taken on a sinister quality.

Calloway wasn't alone in the office. With him was the ever-smiling Colonel Slade and another man, equally distinctive. Somehow Slade and this man who turned out to be James Yeager had the look of fine character actors in technicolor. Yeager, described by Mike McCormick as the expert on foreign diplomacy, had the same deep tan as Slade. Quist wondered if they shared the same sunlamp. Yeager was very mod as opposed to Slade's close-cropped military look. Prematurely white hair was worn long and expertly styled. The finely-boned face had been etched by sardonic lines. This man, Quist thought, had been laughing at fools all of his life. He was aware of being instantly measured. Yeager was making a judgment on how clever he had to be in dealing with Quist.

"Well, Mr. Quist, are you satisfied?" Calloway asked. He was seated at the desk. Slade sat in an armchair to one side of it. Yeager stood by the windows overlooking the ocean.

"I am satisfied that the man I've just seen could be Barney Steel," Quist said.

"Could be?" Yeager asked, in an amused tone.

"He is closer to being Barney Steel than your man Drysdale," Quist said.

"I'm sorry that you aren't totally convinced," Yeager said. "It would make what comes next easier."

"What comes next?"

Calloway reached out a pudgy hand and touched the intercom box on his desk. "We have, of course, heard your entire conversation with Barney," he said. "So we know that he has explained to you that we have problems with which you must help us."

"Must?" Quist said.

"Must," Colonel Slade said.

"Until you began to spread the word that something had happened to Barney, that he was dead or held prisoner by some mythical villains," Yeager said, "all we needed from you was your expert and perfectly honest services to promote the Steel Palace. Now that you have spread false rumors we need you to help undo them in a not quite so honest fashion."

"I have been feeling threatened for the last half hour, Yeager," Quist said. "I don't like it. What is it you want me to do—that I 'must' do?"

"Oh, you must, you know, Mr. Quist. You really must," Slade said, the white smile painted on his face.

"To begin with, Mr. Quist, you will be our guest for the next twelve days—until after the grand opening has successfully taken place."

"That's out of the question," Quist said. "I have a business to carry on. I have other clients besides the Steel Palace."

"I think you will stay," Calloway said.

Quist felt the pulse throbbing at his temples. "You propose to lock me up in the attic along with your Barney Steel and his doubles?"

"Oh no, Mr. Quist," Yeager said cheerfully. "We expect you to be very visible, very available to the public, the press, our guests."

"That should be pretty hard to manage if I choose not to," Quist said. "And don't mention money to me. I don't have a price."

"You will bring help down here from your office, if you need it," Yeager said. "You will issue daily releases to the press about the daily doings of Barney Steel."

"How many peanut butter and jelly sandwiches he's eaten?" Quist asked.

Yeager's chuckle let it be known that he was a man who appreciated a wisecrack. "I suggest something a little more glamorous than that. We will provide you with interesting comments on world affairs, economic forecasts, and a fortuitous word here and there about the Steel Palace and its upcoming grand opening."

"The media isn't going to be thrilled by that kind of garbage," Quist said.

"I think we'll have no trouble with the media," Calloway said. "I won't take the time now to give you a list of Barney's holdings in television, radio, and newspapers here and abroad. They will take news items about Barney."

"Especially under the by-line of the famous Julian Quist," Yeager said. "We have it in mind that your lady—your associate—Miss Morton be brought into the picture. Her recent brilliant article on women executives in *Newsview Magazine* enhances her by-line, and she should be marvelous at providing the public with the glamorous woman's angle on Barney's day-to-day activities as he prepares to entertain almost all the money in the world at the opening of the Palace." Yeager laughed. " 'At breakfast with Barney Steel on the terrace of his fabulous new gambling resort in Atlantic City, he told me—' That sort of thing, Quist, fed out every day, may put out the fire we talked about."

"Miss Morton's presence here should make your stay with us pleasanter, I should think," Calloway said.

"The reason my name has some value with the media," Quist said, his voice quiet in spite of his anger, "is that I never hand them anything that isn't, to the best of my knowledge, the truth."

"Precisely your value to us," Yeager said.

"I don't intend to hand out phony releases for anyone, not

for any amount of money," Quist said.

"There are other ways to persuade you to do what we want," Slade said. He looked at the other two men. "Hasn't the time come to turn on the heat?" he asked.

"I've had enough of this," Quist said. He turned, as if to leave, knowing that he wasn't going to make it. Mulloy stood with his back to the office door, his right hand under the left lapel of his coat in the neighborhood of the bulging holster.

"Wait just a minute, Quist," Yeager said cheerfully. "There just is no way for you to say no to this proposition. We can't let you say no. So we have to take extreme measures."

"Call your Miss Morton in New York," Slade said. "At your apartment, not the office."

"Why should I?" Quist asked.

"To find out just how hot the heat is," Slade said. "After that we can go into details."

Calloway pushed the white telephone across the desk top toward Quist.

"You bastards!" Quist said very softly.

He dialed his home number in New York. On the second ring Lydia answered.

"You ought to be at the office," Quist said.

"I know. Oh, Julian, are you all right?"

"In a manner of speaking," Quist said. "And you?"

"In a manner of speaking."

"You're not alone?"

"No."

"Who?"

"A man who said he had a message from you. And then there turned out to be two men."

"Have they hurt you in any way?"

"No. Most polite. But it seemed wise to do what they said,

which was to wait for a call from you."

Slade's hand closed over Quist's wrist. "Tell her you'll call back in a few minutes," he said, the white smile missing.

"I had to find out just what your situation is," Quist said to Lydia. "I'll call you back presently."

"Oh, Julian!"

"Keep your powder dry," Quist said and put down the phone. He looked at Slade, his eyes cold as two newly minted dimes. "If anything happens to her, Slade, I promise you—"

"Oh for God sake, let's not waste time with schoolboy boasts," Slade interrupted. "We hold all the cards, have all the power. You and Miss Morton can come out of this in one piece if you don't act like a damn fool."

"It's all so simple," Yeager said. "You will call Miss Morton back and tell her to pack for an extended stay. Perhaps she can also pack for you. Our men will fly her down here in one of Barney's planes and deliver her to you here without one hair of her lovely head being ruffled—unless you make mistakes, Mr. Quist. You will be perfectly safe here, free as a bird—unless she makes mistakes. Once she arrives, you will be given one of the best suites in the Palace as Barney's guests. You will dine and wine in luxury. Your only responsibility will be to deal with the media on a daily basis, make it perfectly clear to the world that Barney is alive and well and looking forward to the arrival of his guests from all over the globe."

"Free as a bird, you say," Quist said. "But we will not be allowed to leave the hotel, not be allowed to use a telephone to call my office and explain my absence. One of your hit men will have a gun at our backs wherever we go. And when the party is over, if we tell the truth about what's gone on here? What then?"

"After the party is over we'll simply laugh at rumors of that sort," Yeager said. "But of course you'll be allowed to use the phone to call your office, or anyone else you like. Of course all your calls will be monitored. If you choose to leave the hotel, even go back to New York for business reasons, Miss Morton will be here to guarantee your return. If you want to send her somewhere, you will be here to guarantee her return. It can all be so simple, so pleasant. You've seen Barney. You know he's alive. You're not covering up a murder as you seem to have imagined when you talked to Mike McCormick."

"How do you know what I said to Mike McCormick if he never got here to the Palace?" Quist asked.

"I knew what you had said to him the day before yesterday when I came to your office," Slade said. "That was less than an hour after you'd said it."

It was just possible, Quist thought. For some reason Mike McCormick's apartment could have been bugged. Barney Steel's security people probably violated a thousand privacies. Mike had known so much about Barney's past they may have considered him a risk.

In New York two men were sitting in his apartment with Lydia, and Quist guessed that if he refused flatly to do what he was told, these men, who thought of themselves as all powerful and untouchable, would bring him to his knees by inflicting some kind of violence on her. Better to get her here and to play along until he could figure some way out. He faced the three men who were in effect his jailers.

"As you say, you hold all the cards, have all the power," he said. "I don't have much choice."

"No choice at all," Slade said.

"So I call Lydia and tell her to pack for us both and come down here with your men. May she call the office and tell them that we won't be there for a few days?"

"My dear fellow, you may call the office yourself," Yeager said. "Now, we have set up a press office for you in the ballroom. I hope you'll find everything you need. I think you should get to your first release. Your meeting with Barney as you take on the P.R. job should do, shouldn't it? You will color it, of course. A literal description of Barney as he is would hardly do. Then when Miss Morton gets here we will let her choose a suite of rooms for you that pleases her. We want you to be comfortable and happy."

"There is a legal term applied to unfriendly witnesses which describes what I am, Yeager," Quist said. "The term is 'hostile.' "

2

He was, in effect, a prisoner in a jail that had no bars on the windows, no locks on the doors. He could walk out the front door and call the nearest cop, and while he tried to prove that he was being held against his will, coerced into doing something he didn't want to do, two men in New York would make Lydia pay for his folly. He would then charge them with a crime and could hear himself being laughed out of court. He could hear the sardonic James Yeager suggesting that this man Quist was just slightly mad. He had spread rumors that Barney Steel was dead or a prisoner, and they could produce Barney Steel to refute that charge. Kidnaped or killed or tortured his girl friend? How utterly absurd. Raising an uproar about Barney Steel and his Big Five would be an inconvenience to them, but he would have no proof, and it would be too late to undo whatever they had in mind for Lydia. He would have to admit that his earlier concerns for Barney Steel were probably unfounded. He had seen the real Steel now, amputated finger and all. At this moment he held nothing but losing cards.

First things first. He must get Lydia down here to the Steel Palace where he had at least a chance to protect her.

Mulloy guided him across the lobby to the office they had prepared for him. These people did nothing by halves. It was a bright sunlit room overlooking the ocean. It was furnished more like a man's study in his home than an office; a flat-topped desk, comfortable leather armchairs, bookcases filled with books which looked as if they'd never been read. There was a typewriter on a movable stand, a tape recorder on the desk. There was a telephone. And there was a secretary!

"My name is Joy Holliday," a pert little blonde girl told him. "Mr. Calloway has assigned me to be your secretary while you're here, Mr. Quist."

He sat down in the Windsor armchair behind the desk. He could pick up the phone at his elbow and call anybody he liked, but what he said would be overheard.

"I don't really know what use I'll have for a secretary, Miss Holliday," he said.

"Joy, please," she said.

"I am supposed to be preparing some press releases, Joy," he said. An appropriate name for an attractive young girl. "Any writing I do will be directly on the typewriter. I suppose you could make copies for Mr. Calloway."

"I'm here to do anything you want, Mr. Quist." She had a pleasant smile. Everybody at the Steel Palace smiled, he thought, except Barney Steel and the men with guns. "Could I get you some coffee? Is there any kind of errand I can run for you?"

"I have a couple of calls to make," he said.

"If they're private I can wait outside," Joy said.

Either she didn't know that the phone was bugged or she was laughing at him.

"No part of my life here is private, Joy," he said. He picked up the phone and dialed his home number in New York. Joy might as well know that he knew about the bug, in case she knew about it.

On the second ring Lydia answered. "Julian?"

"Yes, luv."

"I was beginning to wonder. You said you'd call right back."

"Everything down here takes time," he said. "Listen, and don't ask questions, Lydia. You and I are going to spend the next twelve or fourteen days here at the Steel Palace."

"But Julian—!"

"I know. What I want you to do is pack for yourself and for me if you will. My gold dinner jacket and trousers, a couple of jackets and slacks, shirts, ties, underthings."

"Julian!"

"The two gentlemen who are there with you will fly you and the luggage down here on one of Barney Steel's planes."

The change in her voice indicated that she was catching on. "Do you want me to call the office? There's such a backlog of things there."

"I'll call Connie," Quist said. "I want you down here as quickly as you can make it, luv. I need you."

"Whatever you say."

"You're all right? No troubles?"

"I need you, too," Lydia said.

That was that.

Quist called his office number and got himself put through to Connie Parmalee, his secretary.

"Where in the world are you, Julian?" Connie asked. "There are people here to see you. You've already missed two appointments."

"I'm at the Steel Palace in Atlantic City," Quist said.

"Why didn't you tell me? I could have canceled appointments instead of having people swarm in here."

"Couldn't be helped," Quist said. "It gets worse, Connie. Lydia and I will be down here for the next twelve days at least.

You'll have to bury yourself in apologies and rearrangements."

"It's just not that simple, Julian. I—"

"One important thing," Quist said. "Tell Dan Garvey I want him to take charge, personally, of the Snowden account."

"The Snowden account?"

"Yes, Connie. The Snowden account."

There was a moment's hesitation and then Connie said: "I'll tell Dan."

"Good girl."

"Is it possible for Dan to reach you down there—in case he needs you?"

"Any time, day or night," Quist said. "I even have my own phone."

"Take care, Julian."

"Do my best," he said.

"I'm just quoting what he said to me on the phone," Connie Parmalee said to Dan Garvey. They were in Garvey's office at Julian Quist Associates in New York.

"What the hell is the Snowden account?" Garvey asked, scowling. The word that Quist and Lydia might be gone for as much as two weeks was disturbing. The business didn't operate too well without Quist at the wheel.

"I don't know what the Snowden account is," Connie said.

"Didn't you ask?"

"No, I didn't. There was something odd about the whole conversation."

"Odd?"

"I can't explain, Dan. Julian didn't sound like himself. I thought 'the Snowden account' might mean something to you. I thought maybe it was some kind of a message to you. Is Julian involved with some other girl?"

"No such luck," Garvey said. Lydia was still under his skin.

"I had the feeling Julian wasn't alone. That there was someone there listening. Do you suppose—"

"Snowden!" Garvey said, bringing the flat of his hand down on his desk. "Wasn't that a homicide that Mark Kreevich handled? A banker who was murdered in his Park Avenue apartment a couple of months ago?"

"I seem to remember—"

"He wants me to get in touch with Kreevich!" Garvey said. "See if you can get him on the phone."

An hour later Lieutenant Kreevich, reached on the phone, walked into Garvey's office. The homicide man listened to Connie's account of Quist's call.

"The Snowden case was locked up and put to bed weeks ago," he said. "The killer comes to trial in another ten days. No connection with Julian in any way. But, I think he must have meant you to call me. I'm not sure I'm smart enough to know why."

"He told you about the Steel Palace deal," Garvey said. "The stand-in for Barney Steel?"

"He told me, and I told him to forget it. But I knew, when I told him about Mike McCormick, that he was on his way to Atlantic City."

"He didn't tell anyone here that he was going."

"Lydia, of course," Connie said. "But he sounded as though Lydia was with him."

"Could be," Kreevich said. "Have you tried to reach her?"

Connie didn't answer, but she picked up the phone and dialed. No answer.

"I'll try her own apartment," Connie said.

She dialed again. No answer.

"The first thing he would have done when he got to Atlantic

City was get in touch with the cop in charge of the McCormick case, a fellow named Tabor."

Kreevich put through a call to police headquarters in Atlantic City and asked for Tabor. He listened to what someone had to tell him, and then put down the phone, frowning. He reached for a cigarette in his pocket and lit it.

"Tabor was taken off the case a couple of hours ago," he said. "He's been given a month's holiday and they don't know where he's gone."

"Is there something screwy about that?" Garvey said.

"Very screwy," Kreevich said. "You don't take a man off a case when he's started it, unless . . ."

"Unless what?"

"Unless he crossed somebody, or was drunk on the job. Or someone with influence wanted him off the case."

"The Steel Enterprises people?"

"Well, not the Dolly Sisters," Kreevich said. He took a deep drag on his cigarette. "If Julian talked to Tabor and got him interested in what he thought might be going on at the Palace, then the Steel people might decide it would be better to have someone on the case who would go along with the sexual pervert theory in McCormick's murder."

"Julian's in trouble," Connie said.

"Big trouble if he plans to stay away for two weeks, for God sake!" Garvey said. "Do you have any idea what his absence means to a dozen accounts we're handling?"

"There's a million dollars clear profit in the Steel Palace job I understand," Kreevich said.

"And it could be handled from here. Better handled from here," Garvey said.

Kreevich's eyes were narrowed against the cigarette smoke. "This is a time to walk gently," he said. "Somebody's got an armlock on Julian or he'd come out with some sensible explanation. No explanation and this Snowden jazz tells us that."

"So what do we do?" Connie asked.

"Smell around," Kreevich said.

Writing a press release on any project with which he was involved was something Quist could do in his sleep. Writing a phony release was something else again. And writing a release that would please Calloway, Yeager and Company was still something else.

Joy Holliday, the blonde chick, busied herself doing nothing while Quist fiddled with words on the typewriter supplied him. The keynote had to be, to borrow from a song, that Barney Steel was "alive and well and living in Paris." Included in this should be some sort of come-on about the Steel Palace, its mink-lined luxury, its promise of fortunes to be made in the gambling rooms. He found it next to impossible to concentrate on what he was doing. At Beekman Place Lydia would be packing, watched by Colonel Slade's two goons. She would be frightened but not showing it. Then there would be the trip to Kennedy, the private plane, the flight down with the same two goons. She would be able to identify them later. But what had they done to her? Brought her a message to wait for a call from her man, escorted her without force or violence to Atlantic City where she wanted to go. Would it be considered legally out of line for Slade to provide security for an employee of Barney Steel? Like Quist, Lydia was in a jail without bars or locks, not pushed around or physically coerced. They were prisoners of a dangerous situation, reacting to what they knew might happen, could happen.

Quist had just gotten his press release rolling when a strange man walked into the office. He was a shortish, square man. In

Quist's football days, one would have said he was built like a "watch-charm guard." Powerful, quick—before whatever it was had happened that made him walk with a severe limp. Like Slade and Yeager, this man was a sunlamp patron, tanned a deep brown. Probably in his fifties, he had the hard, shrewd look to him that Quist had associated with Slade and Yeager.

"Good morning, Mr. Quist," the man said. "I'm Foster Martin."

The third member of the Big Three, according to the late Mike McCormick. Yeager was the man who knew all about foreign countries, Martin was the expert on the American aspects of Barney Steel Enterprises.

Martin gestured toward his right leg. "Gout," he said. "My big toe is damn near killing me."

"High living, they used to say," Quist said. "Ever tried butazolidin? It's a pain killer they give to race horses—if they don't get caught at it."

"It does something to your white corpuscles," Martin said. "I just have to grit my teeth for about five days. You comfortable here?"

"As comfortable as a man in my situation can be," Quist said.

"I just looked over the list of names you brought to Paul Calloway," Martin said. "Extraordinary. You didn't leave out a single American name I would have put on that list. Added some I might not have thought of. Yeager says the same thing about your foreign list."

"I'm being paid a million dollars," Quist said.

"You had help, Slade tells me, from Eric Tranter in the State Department. Smart cookie."

"An old friend," Quist said.

"I trust you didn't convince him of your mistaken anxieties about Barney."

"I don't know how convinced he was," Quist said.

"It doesn't matter," Martin said. "Your press release will clear up those doubts. I came to tell you that we've arranged for a press conference." Martin glanced at his watch. "Two o'clock in the main ballroom. Give the ladies and gentlemen of the media a notion of how they can get rich quick when the Palace opens. You will hand out your press release then and you will answer any questions they want to ask. It is to be your show, Mr. Quist."

"Let me make something quite clear to you, Martin," Quist said. "I can be pushed just so far. I'm holding no press conference until Miss Morton has arrived here and I know all's well with her. I can be more specific, but perhaps we should ask Joy to leave the room." Not everyone could be in on what was happening.

"No problem," Martin said. He looked at his watch again. "Miss Morton should be here by one o'clock. You will let us see your formal release before that time, though, won't you?"

Quist shrugged. "Why not?" he said. "I've always imagined I could have been a successful fiction writer."

"Oh God, my foot!" Martin said, as he turned to leave.

Quist turned back to his typewriter. *"In an interview with Barney Steel this morning in his luxurious penthouse apartment atop the Steel Palace he showed me the list of guests expected to attend the grand opening a week from Saturday. Six hundred of the world's outstanding financial powers will be present. Barney Steel, perhaps the richest of them all, was in high good spirits as he outlined the plans for entertaining his famous guests—"*

When he had finally finished he handed two typewritten sheets to Joy. "Will you make a half dozen copies of this for Mr. Calloway, bearing in mind that I can't spell. If he approves, he'll probably want several hundred copies made for the press conference at two o'clock."

Somehow the spacious lobby began to seem like somewhat less of a prison than his office or Calloway's. The walls were farther apart; he felt less trapped. But almost as he stepped out the door of his office Quist found himself surrounded, found himself in the center of a bevy of giggling girls, all wearing sensational bikinis, all carrying bright-colored bath towels. Quist wondered afterwards if Lamu Sharah selected his wives by measurements. It appeared to him that twenty sets of exquisite breasts were all exactly the same size, twenty tight little behinds all identical, twenty enviable waistlines, the same down to the smallest fraction of an inch. The shades of skin were different, from a rich black to the pale ivory that goes with natural red hair. But the high-pitched laughter, the little-girl voices, were like a carefully schooled chorus. Facing Quist in the center of this whirlpool of lovely girls was the President of Kambashi—if Calloway had been right about the country.

Lamu Sharah was awe-inspiring. There had been something slightly comic about the British army uniform with its medals, but what confronted Quist now was a half-naked black giant, a man with an upper body that would have made Mr. Atlas drool with envy. Sharah was wearing swimming shorts only, but a white bath towel was draped around his mammoth shoulders, and there were white canvas beach shoes on his enormous feet. He towered over Quist, standing a good six feet eight or ten inches tall. Quist had never seen such a physique, neither in life nor in marble shaped by a sculptor's imagination.

Sharah saw the wonder and perhaps admiration on Quist's face and it pleased him. His Jovian laughter set the lobby's glass chandeliers tinkling. He held out two enormous hands.

"Welcome, Mr. Quist! Welcome! I hear you are joining us as pre-season guests. What a delightful surprise. I have heard so much about you, you know."

"Your Excellency," Quist said. It was the title Calloway had given this black giant. He took one of the extended hands expecting irreparable damage. Sharah's handshake was, mercifully, controlled, firm but not punishing.

"For some years past in my country," Sharah said, "whenever I have a project to sell, my advisers say to me, why not import the famous Julian Quist? I feared you would find us too crude, that we weren't yet quite ready for your sophisticated approach." The perfect British accent sounded strange coming out of that beaming black African face.

"That's very flattering, Your Excellency."

"Oh, please, Mr. Quist, since we are to be, you might say, bedfellows for the next two weeks you must address me as my friends address me—except, perhaps, in formal gatherings. My friends call me Mumu, Julian." He took in the whole world with his next gesture. "And these, Julian, these pretties are my wives."

They cooed around Quist like a loft full of homing pigeons. Then Mumu Sharah put a great arm around Quist's shoulders and led him away from the half-naked girls. He bent down and spoke in a stage whisper that could have been heard in the back row of the Metropolitan Opera House. Certainly the "wives" could hear what he said.

"A man with riches such as mine would be churlish not to share, Julian," Mumu said. "Look over my little collection of gems—" and he nodded slyly toward the girls, "—select one that pleases you—or even two. The one—or both—will be yours to command for the duration of our stay here. Your pleasure will be their pleasure."

"You are being far too generous," Quist said. "In any event I am expecting my own lady to arrive very shortly."

"And she wouldn't approve?" The thunderous laughter shook the chandeliers again. Then came a genuine whisper. "No one woman can satisfy a real man, Julian. So when you please, pick what you like from my flower bed. And now! We are headed for a swim in the salt-water pool. Will you join us, Julian? There is nothing so amusing as watching a group of lovely girls frolicking in the water."

"I'm afraid I am preparing for a press conference for early afternoon," Quist said.

"Ah, yes. So I heard. I may even attend. I understand you met with my old friend Barney this morning?"

"Yes." There were evidently few secrets from Mumu around the Steel Palace.

"How did you find him?"

"Have you seen him since you arrived here, Your Excellency?"

"Mumu, Mr. Quist. Please, Mumu! No, I haven't seen Barney. He has, I understand, not been too well. But I suspect he will surprise us all and appear at the grand opening. And now, Julian, my little beauties grow impatient. But tonight you and your lady will dine with me and my ladies. Now, now! I will not take no as an answer, Julian. Shall we say champagne in my suite at six o'clock?"

Quist watched him go, towering over his harem, some of them clutching at his hands and arms, others cavorting fore and aft. It was out of a comic opera, and yet Quist had the feeling that wasn't quite the right description. According to Eric Tranter, Mumu Sharah ate political prisoners for breakfast. Kambashi was a tyranny, and Mumu was the tyrant.

Someone standing just aft of Quist laughed, and turning,

Quist saw a slim, ferret-faced man wearing a gaudy sports jacket and shirt.

"You suppose he services all of those chicks? What a man! I'm Freddy Lenz, by the way."

Here was the last of Mike McCormick's Big Five: Freddy Lenz who dealt with the underworld, the crime syndicates. McCormick had described him as a man with a criminal mind.

"I wouldn't mind helping him out," Lenz said, watching the harem disappear in the direction of the salt-water pool.

"Cultivate Mumu's friendship and you might make it," Quist said. "He professes to be a very generous man."

"Mumu! For God sake, you on first names with him already?"

"I make friends and enemies with equal alacrity," Quist said.

"No point in taking things too hard, Quist," Lenz said. "You took a wrong turn. Keep your nose clean and you'll come out on the main road after a while. Calloway asked me to take you to the ballroom to see if the setup there is satisfactory to you."

Folding chairs to accommodate a couple of hundred people had been set up in the ballroom, a gracious space decorated now with a mass of summer flowers. On a rostrum at the head of the room were half a dozen microphones, each with the name of a TV or radio station attached to it.

"This conference is to be broadcast live?" Quist asked.

"Barney rules the air waves," Lenz said. "Calloway wants you to see if the mikes are set at a proper height for you. There's nothing so boring as a speaker adjusting mikes after it's time to begin."

Quist walked up to the rostrum and faced the room full of empty chairs. A little man in blue coveralls with the monogram of the Steel Palace, like a blazer-patch, over his breast pocket, waited for instructions. Quist wondered if there was some way he could use this public broadcast to his own advantage. By the time he faced his audience Lydia would be here somewhere, perhaps even in this room where he could see her. One false step and God help them both, he thought.

"Everything seems to be all right," he said to Lenz and the technician.

Everything was all wrong, but what to do about it?

It was a quarter past one, just forty-five minutes before the press conference was scheduled to begin, when a black limousine pulled up under the portico at the front entrance to the Steel Palace. Quist, who had been fighting almost unbearable tensions for the last hour, saw Lydia get out, followed by two men. One of the men opened the trunk of the car where three suitcases which Quist recognized as his own were stored. Lydia, slender, lovely, somewhat tentative, started up the ramp toward the revolving doors. Quist moved.

He held her for a moment in his arms, the sweet familiarity of her a restorative.

"You all right, luv?" he asked.

"Yes." Her deep violet eyes were wide as saucers. "What is all this, Julian?"

"Later," he said. He put an arm around her shoulders and guided her into the lobby. Her whole body was trembling.

Paul Calloway was just inside the entrance, giving them a professional smile of welcome.

"Welcome to the Steel Palace, Miss Morton," he said. "I trust your trip was not uncomfortable. I'm Paul Calloway."

The two men with the suitcases stood just behind them.

"I think it's time for you to get organized for the press

conference, Quist," Calloway said. "It will be my pleasure to show Miss Morton the available suites from which she may choose quarters for you."

"I'm not doing anything until I see Lydia comfortably settled in," Quist said.

"Please, Quist," Calloway said. "You know how vital this press conference is to our situation. Miss Morton will be able to watch it on the television set in whatever rooms she chooses. When it's over your time will be your own."

Quist felt Lydia's fingers tighten on his wrist. He explained to her about the press conference.

"The main purpose of it is to dispel any rumors I may have inadvertently started about Barney Steel," he said. He spoke in a perfectly normal conversational tone but Lydia was so closely attuned to him that she knew something was badly wrong.

"Can't I go to the press conference?" she asked Calloway.

He gave her a paternal smile. "I'd prefer to have you choose your quarters and wait for Quist there," he said.

Quist understood the reason for this all too well. If he chose to blow the ball game in front of a couple of hundred newsmen and Lydia was present, they could both walk out, free and clear. Keeping Lydia shut away from him was meant to be a guarantee of his good behavior.

"I think we have to do what Calloway wants," Quist said. He meant exactly what he said. They had to. They had no choice. Lydia seemed to understand.

"Do well," she said. "I'll be watching."

Quist bent down and kissed her cheek. "I shouldn't be too long," he said.

"There is a suite on the ninth floor I think will be just perfect for you two," Calloway said. "It looks out over the ocean, and there is a small terrace—"

Quist watched him guide Lydia toward the elevators, followed by the two men with the suitcases. Anger boiled up in him. The sonofabitch! There would be a time to catch up with all of them: Barney Steel and his Big Five—Calloway, Yeager, Martin, Slade, and Lenz. Yet even as he fantasied a squaring of accounts, Quist knew that he wasn't certain where Barney Steel fit into the picture, whether there was a Barney Steel who still directed his own world. From puppeteer to puppet in six easy lessons. It could be that way, Quist knew; Frankenstein destroyed by his own creation.

People were already moving into the ballroom when Quist got there—reporters, cameramen, sound technicians. Front section seats were already occupied, many of them by people Quist knew personally or by sight. Dealing with the media was part of his business, knowing to whom a story could be released with the best effect, who would swallow bait, hook, line and sinker, who had to be persuaded that a story wasn't just free advertising.

People crowded around him as he moved toward the rostrum, hoping for something off the record, and Quist looked for someone to whom he might tip his hand, someone who might get the true word to Dan Garvey, or Kreevich, or Eric Tranter. He moved forward slowly, searching for that someone, knowing all the time that when it came down to it he would say nothing. Lydia was somewhere, floors above, a target for reprisals.

"I can only go through this once," Quist kept saying to the people wedged around him, a fixed smile on his face. "Ask your questions from the floor, friends."

He finally reached the rostrum and found Yeager and Slade there, waiting for him.

"You seem to have drawn a very satisfactory audience, Quist," Yeager said.

"I haven't drawn flies," Quist said. "Barney Steel is the magnet as you very well know."

"I'm sure you'll handle the situation expertly," Yeager said.

Down on the floor a group of the Steel Palace's uniformed bellboys were handing out copies of the prepared press release to the media people. The hum of voices quieted as they read. And then Quist was almost blinded as the television lights were turned on.

"Any time you're ready, Mr. Quist," a man who was obviously in charge of the lights and cameras said to Quist from just below the rostrum. "Two minutes to two. We'll be live then. If you want to make any sort of preliminary statement—?"

"I'll wait," Quist said.

"Fifteen seconds to air time," the man said, presently, and began counting backwards. "Ten, nine, eight, seven—You're on Mr. Quist."

Quist was good on his feet. He had a gift for talking to large audiences and making them feel intimate. He could make each listener feel that he was being addressed personally.

"Good afternoon, ladies and gentlemen," he said. "You all have the formal press release so that you know we're here to talk about perhaps the most extraordinary party in the history of party giving. I believe there is a preliminary guest list attached to the release you have—?"

"Ali Baba and the four hundred thieves," someone said from the audience. He got a laugh.

"The hundred-dollar-a-week reporter always imagines that the rich have stolen his money," Quist said. The laughter grew.

"I'm not going to make a speech, so the floor is open to questions." He recognized Walter Kellog from the Orange Network and pointed to him. Orange was a Steel-controlled organization and it was certain Kellog would have been primed with the right kind of question.

"The first thing that comes to my mind, Mr. Quist, is the enormous security problem in bringing these people here from all over the world. Aren't they targets for all the kooks and crackpots floating around?"

"I'm told they'll be safer here than they are in their own homes," Quist said. "The expert on that subject is here on the platform with me. Let me have Colonel Slade answer your question, Mr. Kellog. He handles all security matters for Barney Steel."

Slade was factual. The guests would be flown here from their own countries or cities in Steel planes. No chance of any hijackings. The party would not be open to the public, no chance of anyone from the outside slipping in. Slade's people would know every single guest by name and face. The guests would be covered every moment of their stay, and at the end of the weekend flown home, again in Steel's airfleet.

"You must have some hundreds of people on your staff here, Colonel. How can you be sure all of them are to be trusted?"

Slade gave Kellog that white smile. "Screened more carefully than prospective FBI agents, Mr. Kellog. And we have an electronic detection system. No one can possibly carry a concealed weapon, including the guests themselves."

As if on cue a voice boomed from the back of the hall. "Do you think I would be here with my wives if I weren't entirely satisfied with the security?" Mumu Sharah thundered.

The giant black man in his British uniform created a small sensation. There was a move to surround him, to question him.

"I'm sure His Excellency will give you time later," Quist called out over the hubbub. "But we're on the air now and our time is limited."

And so the questions came, some sensible, most of them dealing with trivia about menus, about the gambling programs in the casino rooms, about the small percentage of Americans on the list.

A nice-looking blonde girl in an aisle seat near the center of the audience had held her hand up for a long time, asking for recognition. Quist had the feeling he knew her from somewhere but he couldn't place it. He pointed to her and she stood up.

"Nancy Wilson from *Newsview Magazine,*" the girl said. "There have been some unusual rumors floating around which I understand emanated from you. Rumors about Barney Steel. I wonder if you'd comment on them."

Here comes trouble, Quist thought. He smiled at her. "There are always rumors about men of Barney Steel's stature," he said.

"Rumor says that he may be dead," the Wilson girl said. "Or too ill to receive his guests when they come."

Quist smiled at her. "I can assure you he isn't dead," he said. "I spent some time with him only this morning. Not dead. Not ill."

"We hear that when you visited him a few days ago you detected that the man you saw wasn't Steel but a stand-in or double."

"Bitch!" Slade said in a low voice.

"Quite true," Quist said easily. Lydia was upstairs, surrounded by her bodyguards. Miss Wilson must be handled with skill. "Hundreds of people are always clamoring to get to Barney Steel. It's not uncommon for a man in his position to have a stand-in or double. I was able to detect the fact that the man with whom I was discussing business wasn't Mr. Steel. When I complained I received an apology and an audience this morning with the real Barney Steel."

"How do you know the man you saw today was the real Barney Steel? Couldn't he have been another double, another stand-in?"

Quist suddenly felt his heart jam against his ribs. He suddenly knew where he'd seen this girl before. Nancy Wilson of *Newsview Magazine* my foot! The last time he'd seen her she'd been wearing the trim blue uniform of the New York City police. She was Sergeant Duane out of Mark Kreevich's office.

"It just happens, Miss Wilson," Quist said, fighting to keep his voice steady, "that I knew something about Barney Steel that made it possible for me to be certain that the man I saw the first time was a double. The little finger on Barney Steel's right hand is missing at the middle joint. The double's little finger was intact."

"And the man you saw this morning?"

"Little finger properly missing," Quist said, forcing a grin. "I can assure you, Miss Wilson, and your magazine, that Barney Steel is alive and well and anticipating a sensational grand opening a week from Saturday. And now I think we've run out of time. Thank you, ladies and gentlemen."

Quist turned away from the microphones as the TV lights went off. He could feel a trickle of sweat running down inside his shirt.

"Who the hell is that bitch?" Slade demanded. "You know her?"

"Never saw her before," Quist said.

"Someone from your office must have done a hell of a lot of talking," Slade said.

"I think Mr. Quist handled it very well," Yeager said. "The

doubts came out in the open and were answered. Better than having them smoldering underground. Perhaps it was all to our advantage."

Thank God for Kreevich, Quist was thinking, and for Connie and Dan who had gotten the "Snowden" clue to him. There was a crack at last in Barney Steel's Great Wall of China.

3

There was no way for Quist to maneuver himself into a private moment with the Duane girl. As he stepped down from the rostrum he was surrounded. Looking over heads he saw Miss Duane making her way briskly toward the exit to the lobby. There was no way to stop her if he wanted to, or to call out to her over the babel of voices. Mumu Sharah's gargantuan laughter rang out. He was suddenly the center of attention and enjoying it.

Quist edged his way toward the exit, warding off questions. Finding Lydia was his only objective at the moment. He had to pass close to Sharah in the process, and the giant black man called out to him.

"Six o'clock with your champagne shoes on!" Sharah reminded him.

Out in the lobby Quist found himself confronted by a uniformed bell captain.

"You'll find Miss Morton in Suite Nine A," the man said.

An elevator, manned by another uniformed attendant, whisked him up to the ninth floor. He knocked on the door of 9A. After a moment Lydia opened it.

"Julian!"

He took her in his arms and held her, his lips close to her ear. "This joint is almost certainly bugged," he whispered. "Talk naturally about the press conference while I have a look." He stepped back from her and spoke in a normal voice. "Your two friends?" he asked.

"They left as soon as the press conference was over."

"They must have been satisfied with my performance," Quist said. He stepped in and closed the door behind him. He made a gesture with his hands to Lydia to keep talking.

"I thought you handled it well," she said. "Particularly that Wilson girl."

Quist moved toward the lamp on the center table and bent down to look inside the shade. "She was a new one on me," he said.

Just under the rim of the shade he saw a tiny microphone. He pointed to it.

"Somebody must have done a lot of talking," Lydia said.

Quist had moved to the mantlepiece over a red brick fireplace. He ran his fingers along the underside. A second microphone and he pointed again. "I guess I did a lot of talking about the double after my first visit here."

"You're satisfied that the man you saw this morning was Barney Steel?" Lydia asked. "You made it sound real enough to the Wilson girl."

"No doubt about it," Quist said. He crossed over to Lydia. "Is there some reason we should wait to be together?"

"Julian!"

He bent down, picked her up, and carried her over to the king-sized double bed. He put her down and stretched out beside her, holding her very close. Once more his lips were at her ear.

"Make loving sounds," he whispered.

"Julian!"

"Good girl. We're hostages here, Lydia. If I make a false step, you'll be the target. If you pull a no-no, I will be the target. Incidentally, the Wilson girl is a policewoman out of Kreevich's department."

"Julian!"

"Make it sound more passionate, darling. We're making love."

"In this room, with people listening, maybe even watching?" she whispered.

"Let's hope there are no cameras." Then in a normal voice, slightly shaken. "Oh God, I've missed you, luv."

"I too, Julian. So much!" And then she whispered, "What are we to do?"

"Play it by ear," he whispered back. "One thing's for certain, luv. They won't hesitate to act if we make a wrong move." His arms tightened around her. Then, after a long silence he whispered again, "I don't suppose there's any reason why we shouldn't make love, is there?"

"In this fish bowl?"

He kissed her gently on the lips. "Ah, well, a man can dream," he whispered.

They lay together for a long time in silence, he stroking her hair, her cheek. Finally he glanced at his wrist watch and spoke in a normal voice.

"You have to get prettied up, luv," he said. "We are drinking champagne at six o'clock with His Excellency the President of Kambashi and his wives—some twenty of them."

"Twenty wives!"

"I quote—'No one woman can satisfy a real man.' "

"You're kidding," Lydia said. "I always thought it was the other way around."

"I'll remind you of that one of these days, when you are screaming for mercy."

"Seriously, Julian, who is the President of Kambashi and where is Kambashi?"

"Mumu Sharah is the president."

"Mumu!"

"Affectionate for Lamu. I am on Mumu terms with him. He is a giant black man with a body you wouldn't believe. I saw him in swimming togs. I also saw his wives in swimming togs. Wow!"

"And this—this Mumu is President of Kambashi? Where is Kambashi?"

"Kambashi is what is called a 'newly emerging nation' in what was once the Congo," Quist said. "Mumu is the president, which is a synonym for dictator, tyrant. He has murdered several thousand of his political enemies—like for breakfast. Incidentally, he eats a four-pound rib roast of beef for breakfast along with side dishes."

"My God!" Lydia said. "Why are we drinking with him?"

"And dining," Quist said. "Because you and I and Mumu and his dolls are the only guests in the Palace at the moment."

"We are *guests?*"

Quist glanced at the table lamp with its hidden microphone. "It's a polite way of describing our situation," he said.

The squawk box on the desk in Quist's office in New York was open. Gathered around it were Dan Garvey, Connie Parmalee, Quist's secretary, Bobby Hilliard, the young Jimmy Stewart associate, and Lieutenant Kreevich of Homicide. Coming through the box on a telephone call was the crisp young voice of Sergeant Nancy Duane, calling from a pay phone in Atlantic City.

"I put it on as heavily as I dared," Nancy Duane said.

"We were all watching. You did fine, Sergeant," Kreevich said. "Do you think Quist recognized you out of uniform?"

"I had a feeling he did, but I can't be sure. He played it very cool."

"He sure did."

"I don't know how to make contact with him, Lieutenant. I heard Colonel Slade, the security chief, calling me a bitch. Ten to one he will check out at *Newsview* on Nancy Wilson."

"You're covered there," Kreevich said.

"One thing is certain. I'll never get inside the Palace again unless there is another general press conference. How can I be of any use to Mr. Quist down here?"

"By just being there, Nancy," Kreevich said. "You're on leave from your job up here—with pay!" He chuckled. "Check into a hotel as near to the Steel Palace as you can. Let me know your telephone number, and we may find a way to get it to Quist."

"Where do I reach you?"

"When you've picked a place and have a phone number, contact Miss Parmalee here at Quist Associates. She'll know what to do with it and where to reach me."

"Will do. One thing, Lieutenant. There are more guards than guests or staff at the Palace. Everywhere you turn there is someone watching. There couldn't be an intruding fly without three guys pouncing on it."

"Get settled as soon as you can," Kreevich said.

"On my way."

The phone clicked off.

"I'm going down there," Garvey said.

"I advise sitting tight," Kreevich said. He lit one of his chain of cigarettes, his eyes narrowed against the smoke. "Julian will be in touch when he can. Barge in down there and you may screw up something he's worked out for himself."

Garvey brought his fist down on the desk top in front of him. "What the hell are they up to, Mark? So Julian was wrong and Barney Steel is okay. Why have they got Julian and Lydia locked in—because it amounts to that, doesn't it? That press conference should have reassured anyone who had been disturbed by the rumors Julian started. Why do they need to keep him—and Lydia—there?"

"If Julian steps out of line, they've got Lydia to twist his arm with. And vice versa."

"It's not a matter of life or death if some rich Arab oil man decides not to attend the opening, is it?" Garvey said. "They've got more names on that list than they can take care of at the Palace. So somebody doesn't come, somebody else will. Why do they have to keep Julian there?"

"Because once he's out of there and free, he may know something that will blow the whole thing," Kreevich said.

"So will they let him go afterwards if he can tell something that will damage them—tell that he was held prisoner there—what the real truth is about Barney Steel?"

"We have twelve days," Kreevich said.

"Hopefully," Garvey said. "If somebody makes a wrong move who can say how long we've got?"

"So let's be sure we don't make it," Kreevich said. "Julian may find a way to clue us in."

"He better do it damned soon," Garvey said. "There's no way to help him from here."

* * *

It was a not quite believable evening, from start to alarming finish. At a few minutes past six Quist and Lydia took an elevator to the fourteenth floor where His Excellency, the president of Kambashi, had three adjoining suites to take care of his female entourage. Lydia was wearing a loose-fitting kaftan, its lavender color matching her eyes. Quist wore grey slacks, a blue blazer with brass buttons, and a white knit turtleneck shirt. Lydia had a short fur jacket draped around her shoulders. Casual elegance for champagne drinking, Quist called it.

There were two men in business suits lounging outside the door of 14A, the first of the three Kambashi suites. Colonel Slade was on the job.

"His Excellency is expecting you, Mr. Quist," one of the men said. He rang the doorbell—two short, a long, and two short rings, obviously a signal. The door was opened from the inside by a white-jacketed houseboy, black as His Excellency the President.

"You welcome—lady, Mr. Quist," he said.

With the door open the brassy sound of a recorded jazz band playing "As the Saints Go Marching In" greeted them. The air was thick with the aroma of some kind of incense. The wives, in bright-colored, filmy garments clearly made to reveal what pleased His Excellency, laughed and giggled as they improvised a kind of dance to the music. Mumu Sharah sat in a massive armchair that looked like a throne set in the center of the room, the girls dancing around him. In a corner of the room two other white-jacketed boys presided at a long table loaded with ice buckets filled with champagne bottles along with plates of finger foods.

Mumu Sharah rose from his chair as Quist and Lydia came into the room. He towered over them. He was wearing a white sharkskin suit with a scarlet sports shirt, opened at the throat.

"Oh my! Oh my, my, my!" he said in a husky whisper.

"Something wrong, Mumu?" Quist asked.

"Wrong? The lady! She is magnificent! She is lovely beyond description! My dear, dear Miss Morton." He held out his hand to Lydia and when she reached out to take it he bent low and implanted a ceremonial kiss. "You make my garden of flowers look like weeds."

"They're charming," Lydia said, surveying the wives who whirled around the hi-fi system, which was marching in the saints, like a field of poppies in a windstorm.

Mumu offered his arm to Lydia. "We will open the first bottle of champagne together, Lydia," he said. "I may use your first name, may I not? We are terribly informal here. You will, of course, call me Mumu." His smile was dazzling. He swept her away as though Quist wasn't there. She turned her head slightly, and gave Quist a wry smile. No woman really objects to such open flattery.

Quist was instantly surrounded by a quartet of luscious wives. They tugged him toward the champagne table. Three of them jabbered at him in languages he didn't understand. The fourth, a dark-skinned lovely, put a warm hand in his.

"You do not mind?" she asked, smiling at him. The accent might have been French. "Mumu is very susceptible to new faces. Your lady is very beautiful."

"And you," Quist said. "All of you. May I be impertinent and ask a personal question?"

"Please."

"How old are you?" Quist asked.

"I was fifteen last month," the girl said. "None of us is over eighteen. Mumu likes us to be young."

"A custom of the country?" Quist said, mildly shocked.

"Mumu's custom," the girl said. "My name is Francine."

"French?"

"My mother is French. My father was Kambashi."

"Was?" Quist asked.

"He was a political enemy of Mumu's," the girl said, quite casually. "He died in the purge of two years ago. You know about Kambashi, our history?"

"I know that it has been violent," Quist said. The fifteen-year-old daughter of an executed enemy cavorting in Mumu's bed!

Mumu was clinking champagne glasses with Lydia when they reached the table. The white-coated houseboys handled bottles and glasses with the skill of sleight-of-hand artists. The champagne was perfectly chilled, dry, an excellent vintage. There was imported caviar, and smoked salmon, and pickled mushrooms, and breaded shrimp in hot chafing dishes. Francine stayed close to Quist, her hand on his arm. He realized, with something like shock, that this lovely child had been delegated to take care of his needs, whatever they might be. There were reserves at hand in case she didn't please.

Mumu, managing two champagne glasses and a plate of hors d'oeuvres, maneuvered Lydia to a couch in the corner of the room. He was turning on his charm like a giant searchlight. Quist reassured himself by remembering that Lydia was quite expert at handling the aggressive male approach.

"Do you enjoy gambling, Mr. Quist?" Francine asked, obviously trying to distract his attention from Mumu's ploy.

"I have never been rich enough to enjoy it," Quist said.

"If you are so rich that it doesn't hurt to lose, there is no pleasure in it," Francine said. "It is a disease with Mumu, and he is very, very rich."

"Roulette, dice, cards?" Quist asked.

"To pass an evening, all of them," the girl said. "It is more exciting when he gambles with countries, with armies, with people. He may lose at the roulette wheel, where the chips represent dollars, but he never loses when the chips represent people." Her dark eyes moved for a moment toward the couch where Mumu was toasting Lydia with his champagne glass. "If you really care about the lady, Mr. Quist, you should, as I believe you say, keep your cool. Mumu can be very persuasive." She laughed. "Mumu is very fond of strip poker. We play it all the time, to pass the afternoons, and Mumu always wins and we girls always lose."

"It must be quite a sight," Quist said.

"If you care for physical beauty," Francine said.

"With so many lovelies to look at I think I'd find myself quite dizzy," Quist said, trying to pass it off lightly. "Tell me about your trip to this country. A diplomatic mission of some sort?"

"So it is said, but I know nothing really about politics or diplomacy. We came here to the Steel Palace directly from the plane four days ago."

"One of Barney Steel's jets?"

Francine nodded. "Mumu went to Washington for a day. Kambashi has a representative there. Mumu is very angry because Washington has not officially recognized his government. So there is no ambassador. There is a great deal of foolish talk, Mumu tells us, about democracy and human rights."

"He doesn't believe in human rights?"

"He doesn't believe you should give your enemies a chance to stab you in the back," Francine said.

"You all seem to have come very early for the party," Quist said.

"I think it was a favor to Barney Steel," she said. "Mr. Calloway calls what is happening a 'dry run.' Mumu is an old friend of Mr. Steel's. I think they thought if we lived here for a while, Mumu would be able to tell them anything that was wrong or would be offensive to people from our part of the world. I believe the largest portion of the guest list is from Africa and the Arab world. Mumu is an expert on those people and those countries."

"And how do you find things yourself? Would you say things were running smoothly?"

Francine shrugged. "Oh, the food is delicious, the wines excellent, the service beyond reproach, the gambling rooms enticing. But we are like prisoners."

Quist felt his muscles tightening. "Prisoners?"

"We are not Moslem women who hide behind veils and spend their lives locked up to please their masters. At home I have my own sports car—a Ferrari—and I am free to come and go as I will, except when Mumu has selected me for special services."

"Special services?"

She looked up at him from beneath her long lashes. "I am a wife, Mr. Quist."

"Ah, yes."

"But here we are not allowed to leave the Palace. We cannot visit the shops. We cannot mingle with American people, who I hear are very friendly and cordial. We cannot even go out on the boardwalk. If we approach a street door there are guards. They are courteous but immovable. Titania, one of the other girls, offered a physical bribe to one of the guards and Mumu beat her so that she is too bruised and hurt to make an appearance tonight."

"Not an abnormal reaction from a husband, even one with so many wives," Quist said.

"Oh, I think you don't understand Mumu," Francine said.

"An understatement," Quist said.

"He doesn't object to our having other men. It creates an excitement for him. When I have been with another man, he makes passionate love to me afterwards—'to win me back' he says. He would even like to watch."

"My God!" Quist said.

"If you were to ask me to go to your rooms with you now I would go, and it would please him. And it would leave him free with Miss Morton. No, it wasn't because Titania offered herself to the guard that Mumu beat her. It was because we may not, must not, leave the Palace."

"How did Mumu find out about Titania?"

"The guard reported to Colonel Slade and he reported to Mumu. The guards are untouchable, Mr. Quist."

That was a fact about which Quist had no doubts. He looked down at the girl and gave her a gentle smile. "You are a lovely child," he said, "but I'm not going to invite you to my rooms, delectable as that might be." He looked over at the couch where Lydia seemed to be obscured by the white-and-scarlet bulk of Mumu Sharah. "It just isn't my style, Francine."

She, too, was looking at His Excellency and a tiny frown was penciled between her eyes. "I understand," she said. "But if circumstances should make you change your mind—"

He raised his glass. "I'll drink to that," he said.

He walked over to the couch where Mumu gave him a not altogether cordial smile. "Lydia has been telling me about your exciting world," he said.

Lydia appeared cool and unruffled, a familiar little smile moving the corners of her mouth.

"Can I get you anything, luv?" Quist asked.

"I think I could tolerate another champagne," Lydia said.

Mumu was on his feet. "I will get it!" he announced.

As the giant President of Kambashi made his way to the

refreshment table to the beat of "Sweet Georgia Brown," he moved in a kind of gargantuan dance step. A graceful giant.

"I am being tempted by dreams of sugar plums," Lydia said.

"I understand that after dinner he may suggest a round of strip poker which the girls always lose," Quist said.

"Not this girl," Lydia said. She reached out and touched Quist's hand. "I can handle him as long as it stays public, Julian."

A few moments after Mumu had returned with a fresh glass of champagne for Lydia, annoyed at the fact that Quist obviously wasn't going to leave them alone again, a maitre d' in black tie and tails, announced that dinner was served. Once again Mumu offered Lydia his arm and led the way to the next suite where half a dozen tables were set up for dinner. The President of Kambashi took one at the head of the room with Lydia. It was a table set for him and one favored guest. Quist found himself yards away across the room at a table with Francine and two other young wives. A string quartette played Viennese waltzes on a little platform in a corner. Waiters came in with a tray on which reposed a whole lamb. It was presented to Mumu who approved, and was then taken to a side table where the maitre d' carved like a skilled surgeon.

Quist, trying small talk with the giggling girls, felt a hand on his shoulder. He looked up to see Colonel Slade.

"Calloway needs you in his office for a few moments," the security man said.

Quist hesitated, looking up the room to where Mumu was leaning close to Lydia. "After dinner," he said.

"Now," Slade said. "It won't take long. You'll be back before your lamb gets cold. I can have you escorted out if necessary."

Quist glanced toward the door and saw two of the obvious security men standing there. He stood up and called to Lydia.

"Back in a few minutes, luv," he said. For the first time he saw something like concern on her face.

Slade, the two security men, and Quist went down in an elevator to the lobby floor, no one speaking. Calloway was sitting at his desk, studying some papers. He was wearing a dinner jacket. He took off his reading glasses and put them down on the desk.

"I'm sorry to have interrupted your dinner, Quist," he said, "but I have news I felt it was important to pass on to you—because of your doubts about us. The man who killed Mike McCormick at the airport has been arrested and has confessed. He is, as we suspected, a sexual pervert, well-known to the vice squad."

It didn't ring true somehow, and Calloway must have seen doubt in Quist's expression.

"Your suspicion of us makes it quite obvious to me that you have thought all along that Mike came here and that, for some far-fetched reason, another of your imaginings, we did him in."

"It had occurred to me," Quist said.

"Well, this news should put that thought to rest," Calloway said, giving Quist a bland smile. The smilers were at it again.

"Is Tabor satisfied?" Quist asked.

"Tabor?" Calloway sounded puzzled.

"Sergeant Tabor is the homicide cop Quist talked to at the airport," Slade said. "He was initially in charge of the case."

"Oh, of course," Calloway said. "It was so apparent to the police that poor Mike had been done in by some sort of sexual pervert that the Vice Squad was called in. They had a different approach from the homicide men's. They, quite literally, have a catalogue of these sexual derelicts who hang around—found an eyewitness who's seen someone on that list, found their man. They also found a gun in his possession. When ballistics proved it was the gun that fired bullets into Mike's head, the man confessed."

"I'd still like to know if Tabor is satisfied," Quist said.

"He was taken off the case shortly after you talked to him," Slade said. "After the Vice Squad was called in."

It still didn't ring true to Quist. "If you're so anxious to reassure me about this, do you object to my talking to Tabor on the phone?"

"Help yourself," Calloway said, waving to the telephones on his desk.

In Barney Steel's world you could buy a cop, you could buy some poor jerk to be a fall guy for you and get him off later. Quist finally was connected with police headquarters and asked for Sergeant Tabor. After some delay he got an answer.

"Tabor's on vacation," the voice finally said.

"Since when?"

"Since today."

"You know where he can be reached?"

"No idea."

"Does he have a home phone?"

"Probably," the gruff male voice said. "But I'm not authorized to give it out. Not any cop's personal number."

"My name is Quist. I'm working for Barney Steel at the Steel Palace. It's urgent that I reach Tabor."

Barney Steel's name seemed to have a special magic. That wreck of a man up on the roof still spelled power to people. The cop on the other end asked Quist to "hold on a minute." Presently he came back with a number.

"I've got no idea whether Tabor could be at home," he said. "He and his family may have taken off for somewhere."

Without much hope of success Quist dialed the number. Instinct told him that Tabor had been swept under the rug. The phone rang and rang and there was no answer. Quist finally put down the phone and stood staring at Calloway and Slade. They looked like the Happiness Boys.

"All neat and tidied up at the corners," Quist said.

"Lieutenant Baumholz of the Vice Squad closed up the case," Slade said. "I have a number for him if you want it."

"There wouldn't be much point in that, would there?" Quist said. "The honest cop is shuttled off into limbo; the fixer is all set to cover for you."

Calloway made a helpless gesture with his pudgy hands. "You're a hard man to convince, Quist. Really, the idea that we're covering up some secret about Mike's murder is complete fantasy."

"It doesn't really matter, does it, since there's nothing I can do about it?"

"Nothing whatever," Slade said, his smile wide and cold.

"Yes," Quist said. Little boy bravado he knew.

Calloway shrugged. "Get back to your dinner, Mr. Quist. The lamb won't keep forever."

What an elaborate charade! A Quist convinced that all was well could be more useful than a Quist fighting them at every turn. So if it didn't work, nothing was lost. So it didn't work. Just as sure as God, Tabor had been bought off, frightened off, and the Vice Squad had been offered a sacrificial goat. The news must already be carrying the fake story. Calloway and Slade probably hoped that Quist's people in New York would buy it even if he didn't.

The elevator took him back up to 14A, accompanied by Mulloy, his shadow. As the door opened, the chatter of little girl voices was deafening. Then the first thing that Quist saw was that Mumu Sharah and Lydia were missing. They were no longer at the head table. They were nowhere in the room.

Francine's warm little hand rested on his. It felt warm because his whole body had turned ice cold.

"The waiter has kept your dinner warm for you, Julian," the girl said. "Come."

"Where are they?" Quist asked, and hardly recognized the sound of his own voice.

"They may be in Mumu's private suite, I don't know for certain," the girl said.

"And that is fourteen what?"

"Fourteen C." Her hand tightened on his wrist. "It's not the end of the world, Julian. A little—a little pleasure. An unforgettable experience for the lady, a delight for Mumu. Nothing lost, perhaps something gained for them both."

"Get out of my way, child," Quist said, and pushed the girl roughly aside.

The two security men and Mulloy were chatting outside the door of 14A. Quist ignored them and went down the hall to 14C. Two more security men were stationed there.

"Sorry, but we can't admit you, Mr. Quist," one of them said.

"I advise you to think twice," Quist said. It was an absurd threat. There were five of them to take on.

"Orders," the security man said.

Minutes could make the difference. He turned and headed for the elevators. Mulloy, mum as usual, followed him into the lift and they went down to the lobby again. Quist charged into Calloway's office. He was white with anger.

"That black sonofabitch has carted Miss Morton off to his rooms," he said. Slade was still there with Calloway. "I want her out of there and in a hurry. Call off your men, Slade, and give me a key to Fourteen C."

"My dear fellow," Calloway said, "I'm sure Miss Morton didn't go anywhere against her will."

Quist clenched his fists to keep his hands from shaking. "If anything has happened to her," he said, fighting to keep his voice steady, "I will kill somebody if I must to get at Sharah. You may kill me in the process, but too many people know I am here and against my will, for you to get away with some fake cover-up. Your ballgame, whatever it is, will be over when that happens. There's no time for you to think it over, you jerks!"

Calloway and Slade exchanged glances.

"I'll go up with you," Slade said.

Part III

1

Slade and Mulloy followed Quist across the lobby to the elevators. Quist had faced danger before in his life but never anything quite like this. This gateless, barless prison with its army of security people, all looking as though they had been cut from the same pattern, shaped in the same mold, was, by the very nature of the slickness of its operation, the quiet efficiency with which everything worked, a scary place. Upstairs, that primitive black giant in his fancy dress clothes, could cart Lydia off to his rooms, protected by Steel's men. Upstairs, the king of the hill sat in his overheated pigsty, eating his peanut butter and jelly sandwiches, perhaps not even aware of how his power was being used, how the whims of His Excellency, the President of Kambashi, were being abetted. And Quist knew he had nothing but hysterical threats going for him.

The elevator, like every other operation in the Steel Palace, moved swiftly, noiselessly, to the fourteenth floor. Mulloy and Slade stood at the back of the car, expressionless as painted masks. Something about Quist's hollow threats had persuaded the security chief to act. How far would he go? There could be only one explanation for Slade's willingness to help. If anything happened to Lydia they no longer had any kind of control over Quist. It was obvious that Quist's cooperation, or at least the certainty that he would not do something to damage whatever their plans were, was important to Barney Steel Enterprises.

As the elevator door slid open at the fourteenth floor, Slade spoke for the first time.

"Let me handle this, Quist," he said.

The flat, cold sound of Slade's voice was not reassuring. Quist had the unpleasant impression that Slade wasn't quite sure what he could do with Mumu Sharah.

The two security men lounging outside the door of 14C came to a kind of military attention as Slade approached them.

"I need to speak to His Excellency," Slade said.

One of the men turned to the door and knocked; a combination of long and short knocks, obviously a signal. There was no response.

"Again," Slade said.

The man knocked again, louder, more insistently.

There was the sound of a lock turning, a chain being removed from inside the door, and the President of Kambashi faced them. The giant black man was stripped to the waist. When he saw Quist the broad white smile on his lips turned evil.

"I will not tolerate this invasion of my privacy," he said. "You know that, Colonel."

Quist charged him.

"Oh, Mr. Quist!" Sharah said.

Quist felt himself picked up like a child's toy and literally thrown across the hall where he crashed into the wall and sank down, half-dazed by the violence of it.

"I'm sorry, Your Excellency," Slade said, "but this particular venture of yours is against all our interests."

"Damn you and your interests, Colonel!" Sharah said, his voice shaken by anger.

"I'm sorry, Your Excellency, but I am forced to interfere,"

Slade said. "I'm sure Mr. Steel, Mr. Calloway, and the others will explain to you why."

"There are no 'whys,' Colonel. I was promised when I came here that anything I wanted, anything I asked for—"

"Not this particular lady, Your Excellency," Slade said.

Mumu Sharah struck the door jamb with his clenched fist, and Quist, struggling to his feet across the hall, half-expected to see the whole building come tumbling down.

"I will not forget this, Colonel!" Sharah thundered. "When you are all in my country, as you will be soon, the lady will be mine without asking, and I will see to it that you all pay for putting me to shame at this moment."

"I warn you against loose talk, Your Excellency," Slade said. He wasn't backing down. "Be good enough to send the lady out here to us."

"I will not forget this, not ever," Sharah said. He turned and walked back into the room, leaving the door open. They could hear his voice, tinged now with a kind of warm humor. "Your White Knight has come to the rescue, Lydia. What a pity, just as things were getting interesting. But there will be time, plenty of time for us. Now, regretfully, I must say goodbye for the present."

Lydia walked out into the hall. She looked cool, controlled, a little pale. She walked straight across the hall to Quist and was in his arms. He could feel her heart pounding. Sharah slammed the door to 14C so violently the walls seemed to vibrate.

Slade, a little muscle rippling along the line of his jaw, turned. "I'll have you escorted back to your rooms, Mr. Quist," he said.

"That won't quite do," Quist said, holding Lydia gently. "I want to talk to Miss Morton some place that isn't bugged."

Slade shrugged. "The cocktail lounge," he suggested.

The cocktail lounge was just off the main lobby, a dimly-lit room. There were half a dozen people scattered at a hundred tables. Quist saw that Yeager was there with a woman who might be his wife. Foster Martin, the American expert, was there with a banker type. Freddy Lenz, the Syndicate contact, was there with a girl that Quist could have sworn was one of Sharah's wives. A couple of obvious security guards were at a table near the entrance. A maitre d' greeted them.

"Give Mr. Quist an isolated table," Slade said.

"I owe you thanks, I guess," Quist said to the security chief.

Slade's eyes were cold. "You owe me nothing," he said.

Calloway, smiling as always, materialized before the waiter could take them to a table.

"I trust you are all right, Miss Morton," he said.

"Let's say the marines arrived in time," Lydia said, still sheltered by Quist's arm.

They were guided to a table separated from the other guests.

"Are *you* all right?" Lydia asked, when a waiter had taken their drink order.

"I'm not sure there's a bone in my body that isn't bruised," Quist said. "God, what a giant!"

There was a small vase of flowers on the table. He took the flowers out of the vase and examined them and it.

"I guess it's safe to talk. Tell me what happened, luv."

Lydia leaned back in her chair, and for a moment her expertly shadowed eyelids were closed. "He just may be the most complex man I've ever encountered," she said.

"And able to break two ordinary men in half with one hand tied behind him," Quist said, grimly. He raised a hand to massage a shoulder blade. He felt as if he had fallen out of a ten-story window.

"The conversation at first was about his beloved country, his

Kambashi," Lydia said. "No flirtation, except in the sense that he was trying to be charming. And, damn it, Julian, the man has such enormous energy that he can be charming. The way he sees himself, he is—is like a hero out of a children's book. He has won his way to the top by sheer physical strength and, obviously, by a total ruthlessness as far as his enemies are concerned. He loves the Kambashi countryside, its hills, its valleys, its plains. He was, for God sake, a farm boy, he tells me."

"What happened, luv?"

"You took off with the Colonel," Lydia said. "We ate some of that monstrous roast lamb. Somehow, I don't have much appetite when I see a whole animal on a platter."

"What happened?"

"You didn't come back."

"I was being conned into believing that someone has confessed to Mike McCormick's murder."

"Oh, my! And you don't believe it?"

"Tabor, the honest cop, was taken off the case and shipped out somewhere. Some sex creep has been persuaded to confess. What happened?"

"I was conned, too," Lydia said. "I mean, Sharah sort of took me over, but there was no kind of sexual approach, no pinching, nothing in the least offensive. Just—just overpowering, if you know what I mean."

"I don't. What happened?"

"He had some color slides, he told me, of his homeland, his own palace. He was eager for me to see them."

"His etchings," Quist said. "My God, Lydia, didn't you grow up on that gambit?"

"I did. I should have recognized it. I didn't."

"So he took you next door."

She nodded. "That's when the whole thing changed. That's when it became all sex."

"Became all sex?"

"Nothing happened, Julian. Look at me! Nothing happened."

"Except he took off his coat and shirt."

Again she nodded. "At first it was talk. There was no use pretending—there were delights in store for both of us—he said. I had, he assured me, never seen or had experience with a man like him."

"And then he took off his shirt?"

"To show me how—how magnificent he was. He—he never touched me, Julian. But—"

"That was coming."

"He's a little boy, Julian. He wanted to win the hard way. He wanted to be irresistible. It would have been too easy to take me by force. That's what he said! But if you hadn't come—"

"You'd have been won over?"

"Perhaps—rather than be beaten into submission. You hand over your purse to a holdup man, don't you, rather than be pistol-whipped?"

"Interesting analogy," Quist said.

Lydia shuddered. "What did he mean, Julian? About being in his country? 'When you are all in my country, as you will be soon—' What does that mean, Julian?"

"I don't know," Quist said. He frowned. "Slade warned him against 'loose talk.' It meant something."

Lydia reached across the table and touched Quist's hand with fingers that were ice cold. "I'm frightened, Julian. Being raped is an unpleasant enough idea, but—but in his own country Sharah would be unstoppable. Why should we be going there?"

"We're not going there," Quist said, sharply.

"If they all say so, then we are," Lydia said. "Isn't that the fact? Is there no way we can get help, Julian?"

"I'm going to try a way. It's a long shot, but the only way I know at the moment. Finish your drink and we'll go up to our rooms."

Frank Devery, the publisher and editor of *Newsview Magazine,* was an old friend. The presence of Sergeant Duane, posing as Nancy Wilson of that magazine at the press conference, meant that Dan Garvey and Lieutenant Kreevich were trying to help. Devery had to know what it was all about. Kreevich would make certain that his blonde sergeant was covered in case the Steel forces inquired about her.

At this time of night Devery would be at home hopefully. Quist had a private number for him and he dialed it when they reached their rooms. His conversation with the editor would, of course, be monitored.

After a couple of rings Devery answered.

"Julian Quist here, Frank."

"Oh! Where are you, Julian?"

"At the Steel Palace in Atlantic City."

"Quite a place, I understand," Devery said, quite casual. "I watched your press conference on television. I hope my gal didn't give you too tough a time. She's new and eager."

"No problem," Quist said. "But I thought I might move her over on to my side if I could see her and give her the whole story about Barney Steel. My job is to make friends for him, you know."

"Can she reach you there at the Steel Palace?"

"Yes."

"She'll be checking in with me in the morning," Devery said in the same casual tone. "I'll have her get in touch."

"You do that, Frank," Quist said. "You really ought to send

a photographer down here. This place is fantastic."

"I might come myself," Devery said. "When do the gaming tables open? I suppose I could lose the magazine in a night's play."

"A few people are playing every night before the opening," Quist said. "Most notably His Excellency the President of Kambashi."

"Lamu Sharah?"

"And his wives. Make your mouth water."

"It'll have to wait, I'm afraid," Devery said. "But I'll have the Wilson girl get to you."

"Thanks, Frank," Quist said. "It might help smooth things out."

Devery was a cool character. Quist was certain he'd gotten the message across that he needed help. He only hoped that the listening ears on the line had accepted the conversation for what it appeared to be.

Quist made gestures toward the hidden microphones and spoke. "*Newsview* could damage the image we're trying to create for the opening," he said. "I think I could charm the Wilson girl into being on our side."

"Good idea," Lydia said. She knew exactly what the exchange with Devery had really meant. Devery was probably even now on the phone to Kreevich and Dan. It was a hopeful moment.

It didn't last long.

Lydia had gone into the dressing room to change into a housecoat when someone knocked on the door of the suite. Quist went to the door and stood looking at the caller, not quite believing what he saw.

Francine, Sharah's child-wife, was standing there carrying a large basket of flowers and fruit which seemed almost too heavy for her to handle. It wasn't the basket that shocked Quist, but the appearance of the girl. Her mouth was swollen and cut, one eye was swollen shut, there was an ugly bruise on her right cheekbone. Someone had given her a terrific going over. Who else but her ever-loving Mumu? Quist could see the child was fighting tears.

"Mumu ordered me to bring these flowers and fruit to Miss Morton with his apologies," she said. The damaged mouth made her speech sound thick.

Quist took the basket. Just behind the girl in the hallway he saw two security guards. He took her by the hand and pulled her gently into the room. At the same moment Lydia came out of the dressing room.

"My God, Francine!" she said. She moved quickly to the child and put an arm around her. Quist closed the door in the faces of the security men.

"I didn't do what I was supposed to do," Francine said.

"What were you supposed to do?" Lydia asked, gently.

"I was supposed to keep Mr. Quist occupied while you and Mumu . . ." Tears got the best of her.

Quist was making frantic signs to Lydia about the microphones. He walked across the room to the television set and turned it on, loud. He twisted the dial until he came up with a rock band. He beckoned to the two girls and they all sat down on the floor, huddled around the set, while a brassy-voiced male singer belted out something about a little boy who lost his way in a big city.

"Mumu did this to you?" Quist asked, his mouth close to the girl's ear.

"I didn't do what I was supposed to do," Francine repeated.

"That was my fault," Quist said.

"I wish I was dead," the girl said, and buried her damaged

face against Lydia's shoulder. "I—I will never be in favor again. You cannot be allowed to fail Mumu."

"Sonofabitch!" Quist said, softly.

"Francine, listen to me," Lydia said. "Mumu said something about our all going to his country later. Do you know what that meant?"

"Oh, everyone will go there after—after they have done what they plan to do."

"Do you know what they plan to do?"

"I said I wished I was dead," Francine said, "but if I tell you I will be dead."

"But you know what they plan to do?" Quist persisted.

The girl nodded her head.

Quist reached out and took the girl by the shoulders, gently but firmly. "We won't be able to talk for very long, Francine," he said. "When all they hear is this machine blaring they'll guess what we're up to. I beg of you, if you know something, it could help us. Because however it looks to you, child, we are prisoners, just as you are a prisoner."

The girl stared at Quist, her one workable eye wide and frightened. Lydia had slipped away and she came back with a wet, cold cloth. She bathed Francine's face with it.

"Many—many of the people who come will not leave when they want to leave," the girl said.

"The guests for the opening?"

The girl nodded. "They will come because Barney Steel, they think, has invited them. But he really hasn't. He, too, is a prisoner. He does what they tell him."

"You know this for certain?"

"A few nights ago, when I was in favor with Mumu, he told me. He was very amused, very pleased with things. Those who are not allowed to leave will be stripped of their wealth—their money, their power. They will give or—or they will never leave. Everything will be delivered to Kambashi, and there Mumu and the others—Mr. Calloway, and Mr. Yeager, and Mr. Martin, and the Colonel, and Mr. Lenz—will divide the spoils."

"And Mr. Steel?"

"It will be too late for him to do anything if he would," Francine said.

There was a splintering sound behind them as the door to 9A was smashed in from the outside. Colonel Slade, Mumu Sharah, and two security guards came charging into the room. Slade reached the television set and turned it off. He faced Quist, breathing hard.

"You are a clever man, Mr. Quist," he said. "Much too clever for your own good."

Quist, who had been kneeling beside the girl, stood up. Lydia continued to bathe the weeping Francine's face with her wet cloth. Sharah, his wide smile glittering in the lamp light, reached down and wrenched the girl up onto her feet.

"You are a bad girl, Francine," he said.

"Let her alone," Lydia said, in a calm, level voice. "She needs taking care of."

"Oh, Miss Lydia, what is mine I take care of myself—in my own way," Sharah said. "You have been telling tales out of school, Francine?"

"She has been telling us that you beat her up because she didn't keep me occupied tonight," Quist said.

"She will regret that she didn't, and you will regret that she didn't—for more than one reason," Sharah said. "What else did you tell our Julian, my pretty?" He twisted the girl's arm so that she cried out.

"Nothing, Mumu! I swear, nothing!"

"I somehow don't see you as a rock music fan, Quist," Slade said.

"And I'm not," Quist said. "You know perfectly well why I had the television set on. This room is bugged from one end to the other."

"What did the girl tell you?"

"You didn't give her time to tell me what day of the week it is," Quist said. "Is there something she could tell me that would be useful for me to know?"

Slade gave Sharah a curt gesture of dismissal. The giant black man grinned at Lydia and then dragged the protesting Francine out of the room.

Slade watched them go, his lips drawn together in a tight slit. Finally he spoke. "Sharah will get her to tell him what she told you," he said. "He has rather primitive ways of making people talk. Since I can't be certain the girl didn't tell you more than is good for you to know, I don't propose to leave you two together to plot something. Gather up what you need, Quist, and I'll assign you to other quarters."

Quist looked behind him and saw that the two security men had drawn guns.

"If I refuse," he said, "I suppose I will wind up dead in the men's room at the Atlantic City airport. Do you have another creep who will admit to sexually assaulting me?"

"Let's stop playing games," Slade said. "You know that we can't have you spreading wild rumors about Barney Steel or the grand opening. We need you, no matter what you imagine, to be openly selling what we have to sell. Miss Morton will be our guarantee of your good behavior. And you will be our guarantee that Miss Morton doesn't try anything on her own. Now please, Quist, gather up your toilet articles and what clothes you need. I'll be taking you to a room on another floor."

The rooms on the eleventh floor where Slade and the guards took Quist was a duplicate of the quarters where he'd reluctantly left Lydia.

"Is there anything you need, Quist?" Slade asked.

"A bottle of Jack Daniels and some ice," Quist said, putting down the bag he'd hastily packed.

"There is a stock of liquor in that cabinet," Slade said, "and an ice machine in the pantry. Yes, Quist, this room is bugged, just as expertly as Nine A. You have a phone, but don't go screaming for help or spreading rumors to your friends. We will know, and we have Miss Morton to use as a counter-weapon."

Quist drew a deep breath. "You are a cold-blooded bastard, Slade," he said. "Well, you seem to have me by the short hairs. I guess I have no choice but to play along." His voice was quite normal, quite cool. "You know I tried to locate that Wilson girl from *Newsview?*"

"Of course we know. Your phone conversations are taped."

"Sounds like the old Oval Office. I think it would be a smart move if I had the chance to persuade her not to write a negative piece about the party."

"Invite her here for an interview," Slade said. "Here in your room. I think we'd like to listen to your conversation with her."

"Whatever you say," Quist said. And then to hide any sign of elation. "I warn you, Slade, if anything happens to Lydia, if you let Sharah have her again, I'll spend whatever time I have left hunting you down."

Slade grinned at him. "A little man with a cap pistol," he said. "Don't wear yourself out making threats, friend.

This game is fixed. You understand?"

Quist understood all too well. Pieces of a puzzle that had been spinning around in his head were coming together into a picture. A deadly picture.

A fifteen-year-old girl, a slave trained only in the arts of love-making, could hardly invent even the outlines of the story Francine had begun to tell them. The girl didn't have the sophistication or the exposure to anything outside Kambashi to recognize a pattern of terror that was taking over vast segments of the world. The hostage as a weapon. Kidnapping as a weapon. There had been more than a hundred Jews held at Entebbe, saved only by a heroic rescue expedition mounted by Israel. Less than a year ago more than a hundred completely innocent people had been seized and held in three buildings only blocks from the White House by Muslim zealots demanding political prisoners, money, control over a commercial film —with threats of beheadings by men armed with scimitars, if their demands weren't met.

What Francine had suggested was far more subtle and complex. The name of Barney Steel had a special magic. An invitation from him to some of the richest men on earth was not to be lightly refused. There would be business favors for those who accepted, and perhaps crippling reprisals for those who refused. The safety of the guests was guaranteed by Barney Steel. But the simple truth was that once these Arab oil kings, the diamond and copper lords, were under the roof of the Steel Palace, their protectors would become their jailers. Barney Steel was not a man in control. He was a prisoner himself of his own terrors, his own psychotic fear of death. Calloway, Slade and Company were the plotters, aided by the monstrous President of Kambashi. Undreamed of wealth would be the price of freedom, wealth to be transferred to Kambashi where it would be split up amongst the schemers. And those schemers would be in Kambashi, untouchable. The governments of the world would shrug off the situation for fear it might trigger an international "incident," a third world war. The millions of lives that might be lost in case of a war would be far too big a price to pay for interfering with a game which involved the rich ripping off the rich.

The guests, unaware of what was in store for them, would come to the Steel Palace, their passports validated by the State Department. The outside world would be kept in touch with the glamorous conclave, the excitement of the play in the gaming rooms. Julian Quist would help paint that picture for the public —unless he chose to turn over the woman he loved to Mumu Sharah forever. All the while, behind this glamorous facade, the key guests would discover the truth. Your money or your life!

Quist's hands were damp with sweat as he went to the cabinet and took out a bottle of Jack Daniels. The ice machine in the pantry plopped three cubes into a large old-fashion glass. He swirled the liquor over the cubes and drank. It did something for the chilled feeling that had come over him.

He took his drink to a chair by the telephone table, started to reach for the phone, and then changed his mind. He took one of his long, thin cigars from the breast pocket of his coat and lit it. He watched the smoke curl away from him.

This was the hostage game with extraordinary variations. No one had to seize a building or the people in it. They had a building. Slade's army was in control and would appear to be the protectors of the victims. They would have control of the guests just as they had control of him and Lydia. If, before the big moment, the arrival of the guests, Quist should somehow manage to get himself and Lydia free of the trap they were in, tell his story to the authorities, Barney Steel and his people would laugh him out of court. There were men with guns? Of course, to protect the guest. Quist had been coerced? A man with a rampant imagination. Wasn't he free and unharmed? The black tyrant of Kambashi had been on the verge of raping Lydia? Hadn't Colonel Slade and his men put a stop to that?

The key to the whole situation, Quist told himself, was Barney Steel. Steel was almost certainly not a willing collaborator. He didn't need new wealth, new riches. The fact that such an elaborate plan was in the works made it seem likely that Steel had managed, in spite of threats, to hang onto what was his. He had probably set up some kind of safeguards that even he couldn't undo. He might have foreseen that some day, sometime, he might be threatened, and a battery of legal geniuses had set up an irrevocable protection. But he could be used to get the guests here who would be the victims. Barney Steel, in that hobgoblin chamber on the roof, must have been aware that the man behind the scrim with the high-powered rifle had him in his sights as well as any visitor.

How to get Steel out of there alive, and ready and able to destroy the men who were betraying him? There was no way to get into that chamber with a gun—if there was any way to get a gun. The electronic eye and the security guards would see to that. There was no way to get to that horror room without a gun without first passing the man with the machine pistol in the lobby, and the ever-present Mulloy with his shoulder holster. You couldn't make a move in this wide-open prison without Slade and his people knowing about it within seconds and arriving on the scene within minutes.

It had been Quist's intention when he sat down in the chair by the telephone to call Frank Devery at *Newsview* and tell him he'd made arrangements to give Miss Nancy Wilson an interview. He hesitated, wondering if Slade already knew that the blonde Miss Wilson was Sergeant Duane? Would he be inviting the sergeant into a trap? If his interview with her was to be held in this or some other bugged room, how could he get across to her what the situation really was? Not in an audible conversation. Not, for God sake, in some kind of sign language. There wasn't even a guarantee that one of Slade's security boys wouldn't choose to be in the room. Maybe he could write some kind of a message and slip it to her.

He picked up the phone and dialed Devery's number in New York.

"Frank? This is Julian. I can arrange an interview for Miss Wilson."

"When?"

"You name it. But it had better be soon. I—I'm going to be swamped with details as time goes on."

"It just happens that Miss Wilson is still in Atlantic City," Devery said. "She's trying to get a complete background story on the whole gambling picture there. I'll have her call you. Your number?"

Quist gave him the Steel Palace number. "Extension Eleven B."

"She'll be in touch when I reach her," Devery said. "Lost your shirt in the gambling rooms yet?"

"I'm hanging in there," Quist said.

He put down the phone. Perhaps he'd be able to get something across to the policewoman. His cigar had gone out. He relit it and leaned back in his chair. Every bone in his body felt bruised.

Five minutes later his phone rang.

"Mr. Quist? Nancy Wilson here. Frank Devery tells me you're willing to give me a private interview."

"Happy to," Quist said. "When can you make it?"

"You name it, Mr. Quist."

He glanced at his watch. It was just past eleven o'clock. "I'm not much of a sleeper," he said. "Would you care to come over here now, tonight?"

"I'm a night person myself," the girl said. "I can be there in about twenty minutes."

"Suite Eleven B," Quist said.

"I'm on my way."

Quist could feel his pulse beating faster as he called the reception desk. "I'm expecting a Miss Wilson," he told the clerk. "Will you send her up to Eleven B when she arrives? You can check it out with Colonel Slade. He knows about it."

He put down the phone. He offered up a silent prayer to whoever might be listening that Sergeant Duane wouldn't somehow put her foot in it when she arrived.

She was wearing a pale blue linen suit with a white shirtwaist, lacy frills at her throat and cuffs. She gave him a bland smile as he opened the door to her ring. A bell captain was standing just behind her.

"Nice of you to come, Miss Wilson," he said.

"Nice of you to see me."

She came in and he closed the door, leaving the bell captain outside. Instantly he made gestures, pointing to his ears and gesturing to the whole room.

She nodded, understanding. Smart girl, Sergeant Duane. Quick on the uptake. "They run a very tight ship here," she said, in her bright, crisp voice.

"Oh? How do you mean?"

She lifted the leather strap over her shoulder and put her bag down on the table. "Insisted on searching my handbag," she said. "Looking for a camera they said. There are to be no unauthorized photographs of the Steel Palace until after the opening. Fortunately I passed the test."

They could have been looking for cameras, Quist thought. They might have found a gun or a police badge. Sergeant Duane had been smart enough to anticipate a possible search.

"You wouldn't have gotten very far even without a search," Quist said. "Most of the largest private fortunes in the world are about to assemble here, you know, Miss Wilson. Security has to outdo the White House itself. You couldn't go into any critical area here without passing the beams of an electronic detector. Carry a camera, or a gun, or any other metal object and alarms will start screaming."

"Isn't that rather overcautious?" Sergeant Duane asked. While she talked her eyes moved quickly around the room, searching for some clue to the microphones she knew were planted somewhere.

"You can't be overcautious with that kind of money on the hoof," Quist said.

"Of course the most interesting person in all this situation is Barney Steel," the girl said. "Is there any chance I might get to talk to him?" It was a question a good newspaper woman would have to ask.

"I don't think so," Quist said. "Someday someone will write a biography of Barney Steel that will curl your hair. But he hasn't given any personal interviews for the last ten years."

"But you saw him—talked to him," the girl said.

"It wasn't an interview," Quist said. "It was a briefing on what my job was to be here—is."

"Is the nature of that job a secret, Mr. Quist?"

"I don't suppose so," Quist said, at the same time making it clear with a vigorous nod that it was very much a secret. "I was to help prepare the list of invited guests. I am to make it very clear through public statements and private assurances that those guests will be protected up to their eyeballs from the moment they leave their respective homelands or headquarters."

"What danger could they be in?" the girl asked.

Quist made it sound quite natural. "My dear Miss Wilson, important men in the world today, men of wealth and power, are always the targets for violence. From Dublin to Angola there are always assassins available. When these men move away from their own protection systems they have to be damn sure of the police, the secret service of another country, or the private security offered. If Barney Steel gives his word that they will be safe, they'll go along with it. Steel's word is as good as his bond." As he said that Quist shook his head violently in the negative.

"Wouldn't the Secret Service, the FBI, the CIA make our own government feel safer about having all these foreign celebrities in the country as guests?"

Quist remembered something like an order that Colonel Slade had given to Eric Tranter, the State Department man. No FBI, no CIA, no Secret Service.

"I think the government will be quite satisfied with Barney Steel's organization. It's famous for its efficiency." As he said this he shook his head again in the negative.

Then he took his hand out of his pocket. In it was a small, folded sheet of paper. He handled it as though it was a bomb that might explode. The slightest sound of paper crackling could bring someone charging in from the hall outside. As he handed it to Sergeant Duane he gestured toward the bathroom.

"I wonder if I might use your plumbing, Mr. Quist," the girl asked promptly.

"Of course."

She got up and walked across the room to the bathroom, closing the door behind her. What Quist had written on the paper would bring her up-to-date.

LYDIA AND I ARE PRISONERS. BARNEY STEEL IS A PRISONER. GUESTS WILL BE HELD AS HOSTAGES AGAINST ENORMOUS PAYOFFS. NO WAY OUT ONCE THEY'RE IN. NO WAY OUT FOR STEEL, NO WAY OUT FOR US.

From the bathroom came the sound of the toilet flushing. If Sergeant Duane was as smart as he thought she was, his message had been flushed down the drain. They might search her again on the way out. When the policewoman came out of the bathroom she indicated with a gesture that the message was gone.

She didn't hurry. She went on with questions that an interviewer would properly ask, and he answered as Slade would expect him to answer.

"I'm grateful for your time," she said finally.

"My pleasure," Quist said.

She gave him a little thumbs-up gesture, picked up her bag, and went to the door. Quist opened it for her and there were two security men standing across the hall.

There was no room to turn around in for anyone. Different guards would probably search Sergeant Duane again on her way out, just to be certain he hadn't passed her any kind of a message.

2

In a glassed-in sidewalk phone booth, blocks from the Steel Palace, Sergeant Duane talked to New York. Connie Parmalee, Quist's secretary, was spending the night in the office. Ten minutes after Sergeant Duane's first call, she had set up a conference call with Dan Garvey and Lieutenant Kreevich. Sergeant Duane was called back in her phone booth and she gave a detailed account of her visit with Quist and the extraordinary note which she had flushed down the toilet.

"The place is an armed camp, Lieutenant," she said.

"Julian didn't give you any more details than what was in the note?" Kreevich asked.

"We were talking in a bugged room," the policewoman said. "He made that perfectly clear."

"You saw Lydia?" Dan Garvey asked.

"No. He didn't offer any explanation, and as Nancy Wilson, girl reporter, I couldn't ask."

"God damn them!" Garvey said.

"Instructions, Lieutenant?" Nancy Duane asked.

"Stay in your hotel room—and watch your step," Kreevich said. "Devery will cover you as a reporter for *Newsview,* but there's a chance someone on their staff might innocently leak the fact that there is no Nancy Wilson there. That could make for trouble."

"One thing's certain, Lieutenant," Nancy Duane said. "You can't just send in a couple of people to rescue Mr. Quist and Miss Morton. If you're going to raid the Steel Palace you're going to need a tank corps."

Kreevich and Dan Garvey and Connie Parmalee sat silent for a moment in Quist's office after the policewoman had disconnected. Connie reached out automatically and switched off the squawk box on the desk.

"So Julian has made it pretty clear," Garvey said finally. "The guests for the grand opening are going to become hostages after they arrive. Barney Steel is no longer in control—if he's alive. We make a move beforehand and God knows what happens to Julian and Lydia."

"If the guests don't come," Connie said. "We have a list. There must be some way to warn them."

"And then what happens to Julian and Lydia?" Garvey asked.

"Suppose the State Department refused to grant these people visas?" Connie said.

Kreevich leaned back in his chair, smoking his inevitable cigarette. "Barney Steel has made a legend of his inaccessibility, his privacy," he said. "The President of the United States couldn't expect an audience. Nobody any longer thinks that special privacy is peculiar. He could stop whatever is cooking, but Julian has let us know he's a prisoner. The State Department won't refuse his guests. The guests won't refuse what they believe is his invitation. Steel owns the police department down there. They pulled an honest cop off the McCormick case. We know that means they murdered McCormick. But proof? There won't be any, no matter how hard we look. And Dan is right, Connie. Our personal concern is for Julian and Lydia. We make some kind of tentative move and God help them. We can't nibble at this around the edges. If we move at all, it has to be one big play that has a chance of winning."

"A tank corps," Garvey said. "Sergeant Duane was right."

"It's an image but not a factual possibility," Kreevich said. "We have to come up with a reality. One thing works for us. Time."

"How do you mean—time?" Garvey asked.

"The guests, who are the key to whatever they plan, aren't due to arrive for days. If we don't force their hand, Julian and Lydia are probably safe for the time being. They are weapons, alive, that they can use against us."

"So we just sit, and wait, and do not a goddamned thing!" Garvey said.

"Who knows?" Kreevich said. "Time may help us develop a bright idea."

Lydia answered her telephone after the first ring. She must have been sitting right by it.

"Julian! I've been waiting and waiting for you to call. I thought perhaps they . . . "

"They don't mind our talking as long as they can listen," Quist said. "You're all right?"

"So far," Lydia said.

"I've just given an interview to the girl from *Newsview,*" Quist said casually. To Lydia that would mean that he had made a contact with the police.

"She seems a persistent type," Lydia said, as though it meant nothing special to her.

"A girl has to make a living," Quist said.

"How long will they keep us apart, Julian?"

He sounded suddenly angry. "Perhaps until they can install bugs in our heads so they'll hear what we're thinking," he said.

"I'm worried about Francine," Lydia said. "She should see a doctor."

"The only doctor she's going to see is Dr. Mumu," Quist said.

Lydia played it cool. "I wonder what they thought she could have told us?"

"Who knows," Quist said. "Try to get some sleep."

"You have to be kidding," Lydia said.

"Love you, luv," Quist said.

She was right, he supposed, but when he stretched out on the bed he dozed off into restless nightmares. And then—then it was daylight.

He lay on his back, staring up at the ceiling. He had dozed all night, fully clothed. He realized that he had slept at all only because he had gotten word to the outside through Sergeant Duane. If, he thought, grimly, the policewoman had made it out of the Steel Palace. He would have to wait for some cue from the outside. But it was intolerable just to wait doing nothing. He was letting himself, along with Lydia and the invited guests, be set up as naked targets for Calloway, Slade and the others. But the odds against any kind of successful counter-attack were staggering. He had grown up on the theory that you always had a chance in any fight; there was always the possibility of landing a lucky punch. There was no way to get lucky here. You might slip away from one guard, but there would be another one behind the next door or around the next turning of a hall. To be caught in a failure meant some sort of disaster for Lydia. Which brought him around to Mumu Sharah. The sonofabitch was some kind of circus freak, circus strong man. To confront him physically was to give yourself the same chance that an ant has under a boot heel. In the end he would be stepped on, like that ant, by Mumu Sharah, or the forces of a helpless Barney Steel. Mumu, and Calloway, and Slade and the others would fly away with planes full of money to the safety of Kambashi, while those guests who hadn't resisted would be left screaming for help from governments that would be helpless.

Slade had said it. This game was fixed. There was no way to win. And yet there had to be! Somewhere there had to be a weak point. A massive plan like this couldn't be perfect. Somewhere there had to be an escape hatch if he had the wit to find it.

He undressed, shaved, showered, and put on fresh clothes. There was a way to get an answer to one question. If he was permitted to go downstairs to Lydia's suite, it would mean that Francine had not admitted to telling him anything, and that they were satisfied that she hadn't. It was a lot to hope for.

He was just transferring his wallet, cigars, and lighter to a clean jacket when the door to his rooms was opened from the outside and a smiling Colonel Slade came in.

"Good morning, Mr. Quist. I trust you slept well."

"I slept, but not well," Quist said. "I was just about to go downstairs and invite Miss Morton to breakfast. Is there any reason why I shouldn't?"

"Yes and no," Slade said. "There is no reason why you can't rejoin Miss Morton, but right now you are needed in Calloway's office."

"Does that mean the girl persuaded Sharah that she hadn't told me some sinister secrets?" Quist asked.

The corner of Slade's mouth twitched. "I'm afraid His Excellency was of little overvigorous in attempting to get Francine to talk," he said. "The house doctor calls her condition this morning critical. However, Sharah is satisfied that she couldn't have withstood his questioning if she had told you anything she should not have. We go along with his judgment."

"My God, Slade, that's a police matter!"

Slade shook his head. "A family matter. In any event His Excellency has diplomatic immunity."

A fifteen-year-old girl had had more guts than any of them, Quist thought. "I want to see her," he said.

"I'm afraid that's impossible. Right now we need you to help with a rather delicate situation. When you have, you may rejoin Miss Morton."

"God forgive me for any help I give you," Quist said.

Slade's smile broadened. "As I told you, the wheel is tilted, Mr. Quist. There's a friend of yours down in Calloway's office. Eric Tranter, your State Department chum. He's being rather sticky about passports and visas, things that are important to Barney. We hope you can convince him to change his mind."

Quist felt his pulse begin to pound. God bless Sergeant Duane. She hadn't delayed putting something in motion.

"How do I convince him?"

"You're an ingenious man, Mr. Quist. You'll find a way, I'm sure."

"And if I don't?"

"I regret to say that matters for you may reach a critical stage."

"Like Francine?"

"Nothing as unsubtle as that," Slade said. "Shall we go?"

The gun-toting Mulloy and two security men were outside in the hall. Quist wondered if Mulloy ever slept. Slade and Mulloy joined him in the elevator and he was whisked down to the lobby. The man with the machine pistol was in place. Bellboys waited for guests to come.

Eric Tranter, looking like an amiable college professor in his shell-rimmed glasses, was seated beside Calloway's desk. Calloway, looking equally amiable, was doodling on a yellow legal pad.

"You and Mr. Tranter are old friends, I understand," he said as Quist entered the room.

"Hello, Julian," Tranter said. "Working down here must be like a vacation. God what a place. I hope to get the guided tour before I leave." Not the slightest sign that he was aware of any difficulties.

"Nice to see you, Eric," Quist said.

It was Calloway's move.

"Mr. Tranter has come here to tell us about the doubts of some of the people in his department," Calloway said. "They feel uneasy about so many important people, so many wealthy men, being under one roof without official protection from the United States government."

"Is that so unreasonable?" Quist asked.

"Perhaps not from Mr. Tranter's point of view, or from the government's for that matter," Calloway said. "But Barney would never allow any other security forces in this building but his own."

"You seem to be facing a dilemma," Quist said.

"I hoped you would tell Mr. Tranter how efficient, how well organized our security is," Calloway said.

"I'd have to say it's quite extraordinary," Quist said.

"I have no doubt of that," Tranter said. "But if anything should go wrong—" He shrugged. "We're living in violent times. If anything should go wrong, if there was some violent attack on someone, and it became public knowledge that our government had neglected to provide protection for the rulers of other countries, the heads of enormous corporate powers, there would be, to put it mildly, hell to pay."

"Can I say that Barney's protection is better than anything you could supply, Mr. Tranter," Slade said. "Let me tell you why. I'm not downgrading the government services, but for a month now my men have been crawling over this building. They know every square inch of it. They know every closet, and cul-de-sac, every fire escape, every possible way in or out. There are alarm systems, electronic detectors. My men know how they work, know how to respond to any kind of distress signal. It would take weeks to train outside forces to be half as ready, half as efficient. We have practiced the run from the airport to this building until my men could travel it blindfolded. We know the safest route, the danger spots, the rooftops from which snipers might operate. They will be covered."

"It sounds persuasive," Tranter said. "How many men do you have under your command, Colonel?"

"Three hundred and fifty," Slade said.

"My God!" Tranter laughed, an easy, relaxed laugh. "That is impressive."

"You see, Mr. Tranter," Calloway said, "the government could be severely criticized for *not* letting us handle the security since it is so much better than anything you could provide."

Tranter nodded and took time to light his pipe. "It comes down to a touchy point, which is where you come into the picture, Julian." He smiled at Quist. No one could have dreamed that he had any clue to what was really going on in the Steel Palace. Yet he must, from Sergeant Duane. "The government, the State Department, would go a long way to accommodate Barney Steel. But, thanks to Julian, some doubts have been raised as to whether there really is a Barney Steel."

Calloway laughed. "Creative people like Mr. Quist have creative imaginations," he said. "It was partly our fault. We have a stand-in for Barney, and we thought we could use him when Mr. Quist first came here to talk about his job. A time-saver, you might say. It's no secret that Barney doesn't like to be bothered with the minor details of his operation."

"I never thought of you as a minor detail, Julian," Tranter said, and everyone laughed.

"Did you see Mr. Quist's television broadcast?" Calloway asked. "If you didn't, then I think he can convince you that Barney is very much alive and in charge of his affairs."

"I know that he is alive," Quist said.

For the first time Tranter seemed more than casual. His angular face seemed to take on firmer contours. "I, personally, would take Julian's word for it," he said. "But I can't go back to my people and tell them I'm convinced because Julian says so. I knew Barney fifteen years ago when he was more public. I think I must see him myself, Mr. Calloway. No stand-in could fool me."

"And if he won't see you?" Calloway asked. "He's a man with iron whims about seeing people."

"If I can't satisfy myself, I'm afraid there may be difficulties about passports and visas," Tranter said.

A man with iron whims of his own, Quist thought.

Calloway and Slade exchanged glances. Calloway seemed unruffled, Slade on the tense side.

"Have you had breakfast?" Calloway asked.

"Yes, but I could do with a second cup of coffee," Tranter said.

"I know Mr. Quist hasn't had breakfast," Calloway said. "Why don't you two go on into the dining room. It may take half an hour or more to persuade Barney to see you and prepare him for it."

"Prepare him?" Tranter asked.

"He's probably very sound asleep at this moment," Calloway said. "He takes pills to help him sleep. It may take a little while to get him in motion."

"Fine," Tranter said. "Incidentally, I'd like Julian to be present when I see him."

"A good idea," Calloway said. "He may be able to use your meeting for another public reassurance about Barney. Mulloy will let you know when Barney's ready, Mr. Quist."

Calloway was smooth. Nothing suggested any real problems. Nothing suggested that Quist was under any kind of restraint. Tranter was cool, too. From his manner there was no way Calloway and Slade could guess that he was here as a result of an SOS. The meeting was over. The four men walked out into the lobby, Mulloy following at a distance. There was chitchat between Calloway and Tranter about the magnificence of the lobby, its chandeliers, its murals, its elegance. In the center of the lobby came a parting of the ways. Calloway and Slade headed for the elevators. There was a moment as Mulloy closed in when Quist could speak hurriedly in a low voice.

"There will be a microphone in the flower vase on the breakfast table," he said.

"That *is* security," Tranter said.

And then Mulloy had joined them gesturing toward the dining room. Even as they reached the entrance to the room Quist could hear the laughing voices of Mumu Sharah's women. The President of Kambashi and his wives were at a long table in the center of the room.

"You know Mumu?" Quist asked Tranter.

The State Department man nodded. "Spent some time with him a couple of days ago in Washington."

Quist looked for Francine, knowing he wouldn't see her. His Excellency spotted them in the doorway, stood up, and gave them an elaborate salute, his white teeth gleaming. But he made no effort to join them or speak to them.

The maitre d' led them toward a table. Tranter, quite casual, suggested a different table in a far corner of the room.

"We are all prepared for you at this table, sir," the maitre d' said.

Tranter looked at him. "Then would you mind taking away the flowers? I have hay fever difficulties."

It was a touchy moment for the maitre d'. He obviously had to make the decision on his own. "I guess we can give you that corner table, sir," he said.

They were taken to a table without flowers—without a microphone. Instantly a waiter was hovering over them for an order. The maitre d' had retreated to the entrance where he picked up the phone on his little reservation desk.

Tranter ordered coffee. Quist asked for juice, bacon and eggs, toast and coffee. The waiter still hovered, handling silverware and napkins. Presently the maitre d' gave the waiter a little hand signal, and Quist and Tranter were alone.

"It won't be for long," Quist said.

Tranter's amiable face was set in hard lines. "Lydia?" he asked.

"We were kept apart last night," Quist said.

"Why?"

"One of Sharah's wives tipped us to what was cooking. You got it from Sergeant Duane, I take it."

Tranter nodded. "Is she there at the table with him?"

"Our Mumu beat the hell out of her. I take it from Slade she's on the critical list."

"They know she talked?"

"I don't think so. She may have had guts enough or resentment enough to hold out in spite of what he did to her."

"Resentment?"

"Sharah was making a play for Lydia."

"Julian, nobody knows quite what to do. Our first concern is for you and Lydia. We have a little time to figure out how to handle the main game. But any visible move we make could spell bad trouble for you and Lydia." He swore softly under his breath. He was looking toward the entrance to the dining room. James Yeager, one of the smilers, was heading straight for their table. "Julian, this building, this hotel, this palace, is the key to their operation. Without it nothing can work."

"What do you mean, without it?"

"I don't know what I mean," Tranter said. He leaned back in his chair.

"Breakfast all ordered?" Yeager asked cheerfully.

"Good morning, Yeager," Tranter said. He seemed to know everyone. Barney Steel Enterprises had had extensive dealings with the State Department.

"Mind if I join you?" Yeager asked.

There was no way to say no. Yeager pulled up a chair from an adjoining table and sat down. He must be hoping, Quist thought, that there hadn't been enough time for important talk.

"Calloway has told me about your concerns, Tranter," Yeager said. "I'm sure you'll change your mind before you leave. We can really handle this better than any outsiders could."

"Colonel Slade is quite persuasive," Tranter said.

The waiter came with coffee and Quist's juice.

"Have you been prepared for Barney?" Yeager asked.

"Prepared?"

"Physically he's not the man you used to know, Tranter. His disintegration is rather shocking." Yeager shook his head like a man who felt a sadness. "It's not, basically, a medical problem. His heart is good, blood pressure normal for his age. His mental capacities are unimpaired." The smile returned. "There's never been anyone and still is no one with his keen insights for business. But—well, he's lost all pride in his physical appearance. You know how he was with women. I don't think he's been in the same room with a woman for ten years."

"Hard to believe," Tranter said. "When I knew him he used to arrange double dates with some of the juiciest movie starlets. What is the reason for the change?"

"A psychosis about assassins," Yeager said. "You may remember somebody tried to gun him down in Acapulco in nineteen sixty-six. Changed man after that. Fear took over. Pride forgotten. He's better guarded than Fort Knox, but there isn't a moment when he isn't terrified that somehow someone will break through the security."

"Then this place isn't as safe as Slade says it is?"

"Nonsense," Yeager said. "An army couldn't get to him. A bat couldn't slide under the door to his apartment. He never goes out of that apartment. He hasn't been seen in public for ten years. He is safer—safer than you can imagine anyone being. But he lives in terror."

Tranter's casual manner was a perfect performance. "It's hard to understand why he plans this mammoth party if he doesn't mean to attend it," he said. "I assume he doesn't, from what you say."

"Not a chance that he'll show himself," Yeager said. "As a matter of fact you and Mr. Quist are the only outsiders he's agreed to see since longer ago than I can remember. Paul Calloway and Foster Martin and Slade and Freddy Lenz and I are the only people who ever see him aside from his personal guards. We have to see him to carry out his business orders. But the reason his apartment is such a mess is that he won't allow a maid or a cleaning woman inside it. He won't let a barber cut his hair or shave him or a manicurist cut his nails. He won't leave that room—except to go to the john—and he won't let anyone straighten out the place. He says it breaks his concentration on matters that are really important." Yeager grinned. "The important thing is to become richer than God."

"He left the room once," Quist said. "He left it while you tried to pass off a ringer on me."

Yeager nodded. "He was there in the john, listening to every word that was spoken. I'm sorry that happened, Quist. We'd none of us be having the trouble we're having if we hadn't miscalculated your gullibility."

"Why do you suppose he will see me?" Tranter asked.

"Because he knows he must convince you that we can handle this gathering of famous and rich men better than you can," Yeager said.

The waiter brought Quist's eggs and bacon. He had no appetite for them but he went about the business of eating. Yeager turned the conversation.

"I'm eager for you to see the gambling rooms, Tranter," he said. "This country has never seen anything quite like them."

"I think the one-armed quarter machines are about my limit on a State Department salary," Tranter said. "Fact of the matter is, I'm a machinery buff. I love to see what nobody else sees in a place like this—your air conditioning system, your heating system, the hundred and one mechanical gadgets that make things work. I earned my way through college as a maintenance man in the law school buildings there."

"I think that could be managed after you've seen Barney," Yeager said.

Mulloy was coming across the dining room from the lobby.

He gave Yeager some sort of a signal.

"Well, it seems Barney's ready for you, Tranter. If you're ready?" Yeager said.

Tranter had played his role like a fine actor but all his skills were not enough to match the moment when he came face to face with an old friend in that superheated, fetid room at the top of the Steel Palace.

Yeager and Mulloy went up in the elevator to the penthouse level with Quist and Tranter. Tranter was given that half-amused warning by Yeager.

"If you're carrying a gun, all hell will break loose. You're about to pass through the beam of an electronic eye."

"Fascinating," Tranter said. "But I'm clean."

The door to the room was opened by that unseen control and the four men walked into Barney Steel's sanctum. The man behind the scrim was there with his high-powered rifle. Instantly they were stopped by a shrill cry from the long-haired monstrosity in the Morris chair.

"I will not have so many people in this room at the same time! There is no way to watch you all. Yeager, Mulloy—wait outside."

"Anything you say, Barney," Yeager said. He and Mulloy retreated through the door that was opened and closed by unseen hands.

Standing close to Tranter, Quist heard the State Department man speak under his breath. "Great God!"

The room was deathly still except for the noise of long fingernails scratching at the board stretched across the arms of the Morris chair. Quist looked closely and saw the amputated little finger on the right hand. This was the real Barney Steel. Finally thin blue lips parted revealing yellowish teeth. It was the travesty of a sardonic smile.

"It will not be impolite of you, Eric, to express your surprise," Steel said.

"Shock is more like the word, Barney," Tranter said in an unsteady voice.

"You may come a little closer," Steel said. "There—that's far enough. You can see me from there. I have changed, haven't I?"

"For God sake, Barney, why have you let this happen to you?"

"What does it matter?" Steel said. "I no longer have friends. I am no longer interested in women. The details of everyday primping irritate me."

"It's hard to believe," Tranter said. He already had a handkerchief out, mopping the beads of sweat from his face induced by the hothouse temperature.

"Do you believe I am Barney Steel?" the creature in the chair asked. "And you, Quist, am I Steel or am I the stand-in?"

"On the only evidence I have you are Barney Steel," Quist said.

"Ah yes, my medal of honor," Steel said, and held up the stump of a little finger. "But I think I can be more convincing than that with Eric. Anyone could have his little finger cut off if there was enough money to make out of an imposture. Eric, the last time I saw you we had dinner with two girls."

"Nineteen sixty-four," Tranter said.

"Nineteen sixty-five," Steel said, the yellow teeth exposed again in that sardonic smile. "The first Saturday in April—a beautiful spring night. We dined on a boat that belonged to one of my associates in Santa Monica. The boat's name was *The*

Blue Dolphin. The name of the girl I dated was Jennifer. The name of the girl you dated was Marilyn. But I wound up in bed with Marilyn, and you wound up playing backgammon with Jennifer on the afterdeck."

Tranter laughed. "I should be ashamed of myself," he said.

"Satisfied?" Steel asked.

"Yes, Barney, I'm satisfied," Tranter said.

"So let's get to the matter in hand," Steel said, the shrill voice hardening. "Why the hell do you want to upset the plans for my grand opening here?"

In spite of the rasping voice, the incredible appearance, Quist recognized the quality of a man who was used to running his own world.

"I needed to make sure, Barney," Tranter said. "There are all kinds of diplomatic complications that could develop with a mass invasion of the kind of people who are on your list."

"You've seen how we're set up here?"

"Some of it."

"Enough? Do you want to see more?" The long fingernails scratched impatiently at the board.

"I need assurances from you, Barney."

"You've got them! My guests will be safer under my protection than you are in your own home. And let me tell you something else, Eric. If you persist in being sticky about this, I will go right to the top. And you know I can. You want to be responsible for these people? Well, so do I. I invited them, I will protect them."

Quist was aware of doubts. This man a prisoner? Francine could have been wrong about him. He could be in this deal right up to his scrawny neck. There was a strength here he hadn't guessed at on his first visit.

"I will recommend that there be no further interference with your plans, Barney," Tranter said.

"I should hope so," Steel said. He leaned back in his chair, watery eyes closed for a moment. "Seeing people exhausts me, Eric," he said. "I'm going to have to ask you to leave."

"I can't say that it's a pleasure to see you this way, Barney," Tranter said. "But I'm glad to know that you're still piloting your ship."

Steel gave them a vague, dismissing gesture, and they started for the door. Then Steel said something that startled them both.

"Eric, I'd give anything I have in the world to walk out of here with you, out into the world again. But it's not to be. It can never be." He leaned forward and covered his face with his bony hands.

"You could shave your head and your beard, buy yourself a fancy mod suit, and nobody would know you from Adam," Tranter said. "I'd even undertake to find us a couple of girls."

"Oh my God," Steel said, his voice muffled by his hands.

Quist wondered if that had been a cry for help. He glanced back at the scrim. The man in the ski mask with the high-powered rifle was aiming straight at him and Tranter.

The door behind them opened and they walked out into the hall where Yeager and Mulloy waited.

"Class reunion satisfactory?" Yeager asked.

Quist was certain they'd heard every word of the meeting through some invisible speaker.

"I think I can promise you won't have any trouble about the guests," Tranter said. His shoulders shuddered as if he was throwing off the oppressive atmosphere of the room behind him.

"I'm sure you have all our gratitude," Yeager said.

They started for the elevator. Tranter seemed to be himself again. "Do I get my guided tour now?" he asked. "I'm anxious to see what makes this enchanted palace work."

"Why not?" Yeager said.

They waited for the elevator.

"If you don't mind, Eric, I think I'll go check out with Lydia," Quist said.

Tranter reached out a hand to Quist's arm. "Surely she can wait, Julian. You have all the rest of your life with her. You can get a good press release out of the magical mechanics that make this building work."

Tranter wasn't just touching Quist's arm. His fingernails bit into the flesh. It was so urgent that Quist looked at his friend, startled. Tranter looked relaxed, except that his eyes were unnaturally bright behind his spectacles.

"I've spent my life waiting for women," Quist said, "so maybe Lydia can bear waiting for me this time."

"Good man," Tranter said. He sounded relieved.

Tranter's interest in the mechanical aspects of the plant wasn't totally clear to Quist, but it was obviously urgent. It was fairly certain that he expected to see something in the cellars of the Steel Palace that would be useful. He had acted his role as a conscientious official, old friend of Barney Steel's, so well that Calloway and the others were willing to humor him. After all, he had removed what had appeared for a while to be a serious obstacle to their scheme.

It was arranged in Calloway's office that Colonel Slade and Mulloy, the silent guntoter, would accompany Tranter and Quist on the tour. The important person turned out to be the chief of maintenance, a clean-shaven, soft-spoken man in his fifties, wearing coveralls with the Steel Palace insignia in a patch over his breast pocket. His name was Conlon, his face the map of Ireland. He was a man who took great pride in the efficiency of his world.

Quist was a man with many talents in many directions, but mechanics was not one of them. Machinery he took for granted, like the car he drove, the plane he flew in, the elevators that took him up and down. He had been known to say to Lydia that he didn't even know how to change a fuse if one blew out in their apartment. Now Tranter's tour seemed to be, for some reason, for his special benefit. Tranter was like a delighted child, simplifying for Quist some of Conlon's more esoteric comments.

There was the air conditioning system, the engines that operated the tiers of elevators, the fuse boxes and electric controls that took up a whole wall of a large room. Tranter seemed to be interested in the huge iron tanks that contained oil for the heating and air conditioning system.

"Enormous storage, Mr. Conlon," he said.

"Takes a hell of a lot of oil, sir, to run these systems."

Tranter seemed interested in some sort of valves at the bottom of the huge tanks. "I don't seem to remember seeing valves like these at the bottom of oil tanks, Mr. Conlon," he said. "My God, if somebody left one of them open, you'd have a sea of oil down here. One little spark—" Tranter looked at Quist, his eyes bright.

Conlon laughed. "No one would tinker with those valves, sir," he said. "They're there in case we need to clean out the tanks at some point when they're empty."

"All the same it makes you think of the possibility of fire," Tranter said.

Conlon was almost condescending. "It would never happen," he said. "A small leak would not be serious, and there is always someone on duty here. It couldn't happen undetected. We have the most elaborate sprinkler system. Where there's flammable material, like in these tanks, the sprinkler system emits a foam, like they use in emergency units around airports, to combat oil or gas fires." He pointed to what appeared to be racks of pipes crisscrossing the ceiling.

"Ah, yes," Tranter said. "And a turn-off valve there so that you can clean those sprinklers."

"Regular routine," Conlon said. "That foam has a way of clogging the sprinklers if they stand unused for too long."

"How often do you clean them?"

"Once a week," Conlon said. "We've never had occasion to use them, you understand, and probably never will."

"If there was a fire—?" Tranter asked.

"Inside fire stairs from every floor," Conlon said. He turned to a wall where diagrams of machinery were posted, along with architectural plans of the whole fire-escape system. "Mr. Steel is very much concerned about fire."

"I should think he might be," Tranter said, "isolated up there in the penthouse."

Conlon pointed to the plan on the wall. "Fire door right in Mr. Steel's room," he said. "He could get right down to the street level without ever going out into the public areas."

Slade spoke for the first time, smiling as usual. "It also provides Barney with a way to come and go without having to encounter anyone in the public areas."

"I understood he never leaves the penthouse," Tranter said.

"Maybe he does, maybe he doesn't," Slade said. "What Barney does is his business, his secret. As for fire—" He shrugged. "Sprinkler systems, fire extinguishers, on every floor and in every room. If you're worried about our guests, Mr. Tranter, I think you can forget it."

Quist, looking at the architect's drawings, saw that the door to the fire stairs was just a few yards down the hall from Lydia's rooms on the ninth floor. It could be a way out, but how did you bypass the security guards and Mulloy stationed in the hallway? Was Tranter trying to get across to him that there was a way out? Not in the face of three armed men. And if there was a way, by the time they reached the street level, down nine flights of stairs, Slade's army would be waiting for them. They couldn't be missing for minutes without an alarm being sounded.

Tranter went on examining details of the system that were Greek to Quist, exclaiming delightedly over the efficiency of everything. Finally the tour was over and Tranter and Quist, followed by Slade and Mulloy, went back upstairs into the sunlit lobby.

"I have to concede," Tranter said to Slade, "that there seems to be no chance for any kind of catastrophe."

Slade's smile widened. "You're a pretty shrewd cookie, Mr. Tranter," he said. "I had a feeling you weren't interested in mechanics as a hobby. The Palace is safe, Mr. Tranter. There'll be no danger to any of Barney's guests when they come."

Tranter smiled back at him. "I'm convinced," he said. "Tell Calloway he needn't worry about my being sticky any longer." He turned to Quist. His eyes were very bright behind his spectacles. "Nice to see you, Julian. You should have a ball on this job. Good luck."

He walked out of the hotel—out into the world. Quist suddenly felt very much alone.

3

No one interfered with Quist's returning to Lydia's rooms on the ninth floor. The two security men outside her door made no move to stop his ringing the doorbell. It could only mean that little Francine had played it out convincingly to the bitter end.

Lydia opened the door. She was still wearing the housecoat she'd had on when he'd been taken away from her the night before. She hadn't slept, he was sure. The dark circles under her eyes indicated fatigue. Her face brightened when she saw Quist. Inside the door he took her in his arms and held her. Words were impossible because words would be overheard. Just the closeness told her everything she needed to know.

After a moment or two he told her about Tranter's visit, told it exactly as it had appeared to be on the surface; Tranter's concern for the safety of the guests, the reassurance from Slade and the others, and finally the visit to the basement.

"He made it seem that he was a nut on mechanical devices," Quist said. "Actually he was trying to make sure there was an adequate protection against fire."

"Did they realize that?" Lydia asked.

"Slade was with us all the way. It was clear enough to him. They joked about it at the end. But Eric went away completely satisfied. You haven't had any sleep, luv."

"Not any."

"So, hit the sack," he said. "I've got to prepare some releases. I may have to go down to my office, see Calloway. Just get some sleep."

"I'm worried about Francine," Lydia said. "Have you heard anything this morning?"

"Mumu gave her a pretty tough going over, according to Slade. I imagine she's in the emergency hospital on the second floor." Quist had located the hospital on the architect's plans in the basement.

"Is there nothing we can do for her?" Lydia had to know that Francine hadn't talked or Quist wouldn't be there.

"I don't think we'd be allowed to if we could," Quist said. "Get some rest, sweet. I'll need you under a full head of steam if there are any fireworks."

She gave him a puzzled look. "Fireworks?"

He shrugged. "Who knows—in this place," he said.

He took her over to the bed, covered her with a cotton blanket when she had stretched out. He bent down and kissed her. And then he whispered, "Tranter was trying to tell me something, but I haven't quite figured it out yet. But there's help outside if we can keep our cool."

She touched his cheek. "I love you," she said quite audibly.

He stood watching her for a moment as her eyes closed and she turned her cheek against the pillow. Then he left and crossed the room to the telephone. He dialed the number of his New York office, his own private line. Connie Parmalee answered.

"Julian here," he said. "How are things?"

"How are things with you?" Connie asked, her voice sounding slightly unnatural to him—but nothing listeners would notice.

"Things are building up to the big moment," he said.

"Big moment?"

"The big shebang; the grand opening."

"Oh?"

"Eric Tranter was just here. He had some doubts about leaving security to Colonel Slade, but he's let himself be convinced and gone off happy. Is Dan anywhere around?"

"Dan has gone south—on the Snowden account," Connie said.

That meant Garvey was somewhere on the outside but in Atlantic City.

"Connie?"

"Yes, boss."

"How does the old greeting card read? Having a wonderful time, wish you were here?"

"You want me to come down there?"

"No, but I wish you were here. There's so damned much about this job I haven't got my hooks into yet."

"Anything I can do to be useful up here?"

"Hold the fort—and say thanks to whoever."

He hoped she would read what he said to mean to get in touch with Tranter and tell him he hadn't quite gotten the message.

But as the day wore on—between the writing of new releases for the press and getting Calloway's bland approval—it began to become clearer to him what Tranter had been pointing at. If he could get to the basement again, there were things he knew how to do, things Tranter had been at great pains to make clear. There was a way to flood the lower level with oil. There was a way to shut off the foam-sprinkler system. That accomplished, there was a way, by tossing a match, to create the most incredible confusion imaginable in the Steel Palace. What was it Tranter had said in an early moment of his visit? Without the Palace their whole scheme would fall apart? Without a place to hold their hostages the ball game was over.

As the idea persisted, the risks seemed too great to take. Getting to the basement was next to impossible. Assuming that he found a way, there would be people to deal with there. "There's always someone on duty here," Conlon had said. And if he could handle that, there were other problems. How did he get Lydia safely out? What about Barney Steel, held prisoner by his own people? Would there be any way to extricate him? What about Francine, in the hospital ward on the second floor? He could hear Garvey telling him to "just get Lydia out of there and to hell with anyone else."

Wasn't it better to try nothing at all? To play the game Calloway's and Slade's way? To let the guests come? To let what would happen then happen? That wouldn't quite work either, because surely Tranter and his people wouldn't let that happen. They would hold off in the hope of getting Quist and Lydia free, but when it came to the last showdown . . . ? Then he realized that Barney Steel had too much on the political ball for Tranter to stop the party from taking place. Without the Palace as a prison for the hostages, Calloway and Company were out of business. Tranter had been showing Quist a way out, not only for himself and Lydia, but for a multitude of other people who were already preparing to walk into a trap from which there'd be no escape if the fortress stood.

The day wore on with the impossible odds against success spinning around and round in Quist's head. He felt exhausted from the simple business of trying to think out a plan.

How to get past the security men to the fire stairs? To overpower them in the middle of the night while they were relaxed, thinking Quist and Lydia were asleep? A boy scout's dream! One unarmed man against two, maybe three, armed men. No chance.

Late in the afternoon he went back to the ninth floor. Two

security men, new faces to Quist, were in position.

"The lady's probably asleep," Quist said. "I don't want to disturb her. Can you let me in?"

The two men exchanged a look, and then one of them produced a key and opened the door. Lydia was still lying on the bed but she propped herself up on her elbows as he came in. The sound of the door opening had awakened her instantly. It could be anyone coming in. It could be His Excellency, the President of Kambashi. When she saw Quist she lay back again, a little choking sound coming from her. She was strung out, almost to the limit.

He sat down on the edge of the bed beside her and stroked her face without speaking. He had begun to come up with a plan that involved her. Could he ask her to do it? If it failed, God help them both. Slade would destroy them both. But wasn't that likely to happen in the end, even if they did nothing?

The inability to talk openly was almost intolerable. Lydia, who knew him so well, was aware that Quist was boiling over with something. She sensed, without being told, that some kind of climax was at hand. She guessed that it was not without danger for them both. For a long time now she had followed Quist wherever he led—questioned him sometimes—but always gone along with him. They had come this far, followed this pattern this far, why change it now? But she wasn't quite prepared for it when, finally, he lay beside her on the bed and spelled it out in whispers.

He was certain that Tranter had been trying to show him how to start a fire, a big enough fire to disturb the total functioning of the Steel Palace. In the confusion and excitement that would follow—if Quist could make it—their chances of getting free would be good. Once free, Quist himself could spread such doubts and uncertainty among the invited guests that the grand opening would be a forgotten dream. Quist couldn't do that unless and until Lydia was safe and under guard.

"Won't they be after us for the rest of our lives?" Lydia asked. She imagined Colonel Slade and his army hunting them down across the face of the earth.

"Not if we can get Barney Steel out and to some place where he can be in charge of his own life again," Quist said. "Calloway and Slade and the others will be the hunted then, not the hunters."

"You're going to try to get Steel out?"

"I have to try," he said, "or they will get to him first, spirit him away, and still be in control of his life and his power and his possessions."

She was suddenly clinging to him, almost desperately.

"Julian!"

"Easy, luv." He tried to comfort her, prepare her for what was to come. "All of that is academic if the first move fails. The first move is everything, and it involves you."

He spelled it out, whispering slowly, caressing her as he spoke. Sometime in the middle of the night, when everything was quiet, she would have to play her part.

"You are going to have some kind of seizure—a heart attack perhaps."

"Julian!"

He put his hand over her lips, because she had literally cried out. She would have a heart attack, he told her. He would go to the security men outside the door for help.

"You'll have to act up a storm, luv."

"My God, Julian!"

While the security people were trying to help her, he would go for help. There was a very good chance that he could make it to the fire stairs.

"And if they don't fall for it and follow you?"

"A desperate man might decide it would be quicker to use the fire stairs to get down to the hospital on the second floor —not wait for the elevator. If they catch me I may be able to talk my way out of it."

"And if you make it I'll be left alone with them!"

"You will recover slowly. They may get the doctor up here. I suspect your pulse and blood pressure will not be normal."

"And if you make it to the basement?"

"If I make it, and I'm lucky, it won't take long for all hell to break loose," Quist said. "It'll be every man for himself then. If they leave you, run for it—run for the nearest way out of this place and look for help. If they stay with you, I'll be back."

"Oh my God, Julian!"

"I shouldn't ask you," he said. "But it's not for me or you. It's for Barney Steel and for hundreds of people who are walking into a black disaster."

"Why us, Julian? If Eric Tranter knows the trouble we're in, why doesn't he bring help in to get us?"

"Because he would find us dead, caught in some kind of crossfire."

They lay still for a long time, holding each other. Finally Lydia turned her face on the pillow to look at him. "If you say this is the only way, Julian, I'll throw the biggest fit you ever saw."

He cupped her face in his hands and kissed her gently. Then he spoke in a loud clear voice. "I'm beginning to dream of some kind of dinner, Lydia. Shall we have it here in our rooms?"

Time seemed to drag like a load of iron. They ordered a light supper, talking about nothing that mattered as they were expertly served. Finally, shortly after nine o'clock the room service waiter took away the table and the service and they were alone. After midnight was to be the time. Quist walked over to the television set and turned the switch. Nothing happened. It didn't work. Slade had seen to that. There'd be no covering up of conversations.

The waiting was almost unbearable. Half a dozen times Quist changed his mind. He couldn't ask Lydia to do this. The odds against a complete success were so great. Suppose he did make it to the fire stairs and to the basement and found himself caught off base there? It had been made perfectly clear to him that Lydia would pay the price for any overt act of his. There was no doubt Slade would carry out his threat. There was too much at stake for them.

About eleven o'clock he walked over to where she was sitting in the yellow light from a table lamp, staring straight ahead of her at nothing—or at a vision of what might happen, what might go wrong. One of the microphones was on the underside of that lampshade. He made a gesture with his hands indicating that everything was off. She looked straight at him.

"I'm not feeling very well, Julian," she said. "If you'll excuse me I think I'll lie down for a bit."

He followed her to the bed, kneeled down beside her.

"I'm not going through with it," he whispered.

"You have to," she said. "If there was any other way you'd have thought of it."

"The risk is too great."

"The risk of doing nothing is too great," she whispered. "Just tell me when, Julian." Then she made a little moaning sound. "I have an awfully tight feeling in my chest," she said out loud.

It was a strange business. She would smile at him and then make a little sound of being in pain.

"Is there something I can do for you?" he asked, aloud.

"I don't think so, luv. It's probably just a little indigestion. It'll go away."

An hour went by, punctured by these little interruptions of

faint discomfort from Lydia. Finally at about a quarter to one he knelt down beside her again. "We can still call it off," he whispered.

"Let's get it over with," she said. "Now?"

He nodded.

"I love you, Julian."

"I love you, my darling." Cliché words, but they were his whole life—what was left of it.

Lydia screamed, a shrill, piercing scream. It was a fake but it turned Quist's blood cold.

"Lydia, what is it?"

"I—I can't breathe!" she said. "Oh my God, Julian!" And she screamed again.

Quist went to the door and wrenched it open. The two security men were standing there at attention, having heard the commotion. Thank God Mulloy was missing. He did have to sleep sometime.

"I need help!" Quist said. "The lady's having a heart attack, I think."

They had heard it coming for some time now. The instinct to help someone in distress was strong, even with paid killers. Lydia was lying white and still on the bed now.

"I don't think she's breathing," one of the men said.

"Try mouth-to-mouth," the other one suggested. They were genuinely concerned.

"God damn it, I'm going to get proper help!" Quist shouted, and ran out into the hall.

The fire door wasn't more than three yards away. He reached it, wrenched it open, took a quick look over his shoulder, and plunged into a dimly lit cement-lined stairway. He ran down, down, flight after flight, expecting to be confronted at each landing by more of Slade's men. No one appeared. So far it was working. Breathless, he reached a landing with a red sign over a door. STREET EXIT. There was further to go, down to the basement.

He moved slowly now, needing to catch his breath, fearing that the clatter of his heels on the cement steps might be heard. "There is always someone on duty here," Conlon had said. One or more than one?

There was a sign over another door. MAINTENANCE. Would it be locked? Would it open with a noisy squeaking that would alert whoever was on the other side of it?

He tried it. It pulled outward toward him. It would naturally be that way in case men in the basement needed to escape. The steady noise of the air conditioning machines which came to him as the door opened, covered any sound it might make. He stood inside, fighting for breath. He moved a little further out into the open. He saw the door to a small office standing open. In the light from a naked bulb he saw a man, sitting at a table, with a Thermos of coffee beside him. He was reading a magazine of some sort, his back to Quist.

Quist moved quickly. Had the men upstairs given the alarm, or did they assume he'd gone to the hospital on the second floor for help? Commando experience in the marines, long ago, had taught him things. Silently he crept up behind the watchman and brought the edge of his hand down on the man's neck in a powerful, chopping blow. The man half-rose in his chair and then toppled over onto the floor, the chair splintering under him.

Quist hurried out to the maintenance room. His first attention was to the foam sprinkler. He found the turn-off handle and closed it tight. Then he went to one of the huge oil tanks. There was that valve for cleaning purposes at the bottom. The damn thing was stuck tight, probably rusted shut. He applied all the pressure he could, sweat running down his face. He couldn't come this far and fail. He looked around and saw a tin box of tools lying across the way. He got to it and found a hammer. From there he could see the man in the office, lying still as a corpse.

He got back to the valve on the oil tank and pounded at it. He thought it sounded like a giant gong. If there was anyone else on this level it would bring them on the run. He tried again to open the valve, banged at it again with the hammer, tried again—and it opened like the top on a medicine bottle. A thick stream of oil cascaded out onto the floor.

Quist turned toward the fire stairs again and stopped. He couldn't leave that man in the office. He ran to him, took him under the arms, and dragged him toward the fire stairs. The oil was spreading rapidly all across the stone floor. Quist got his man to the fire door, pushed it open, and dragged the man through to the cement-lined stairway.

Then he turned back.

The smell of the spreading oil was pungent. He took his handkerchief out of his pocket and his cigar lighter. The flame from the lighter set the handkerchief to burning. What had Tranter said? There'd be a sea of oil if that valve was opened. He tossed the burning handkerchief down the two steps to that sea, and then slammed the fire door closed. He heard the roar of sudden flames.

He pulled the unconscious man up a few steps and left him there. Then he headed up for the lobby level.

The air was still fresh in the fire stair. It was tightly sealed off from the rest of the building. But it was something else in the lobby. Smoke was pouring up through the elevator shafts. The fire in the basement was already a roaring inferno. The confusion was total.

Quist saw Paul Calloway standing, white-faced, in his office door. Slade was at the reception desk, trying desperately to reach someone on a telephone there. The man with the machine pistol who guarded the private elevator leading to Barney Steel's apartment, had backed away from his post, coughing and choking. There was suddenly the shrill sound of fire alarms going off all over the building. Quist heard the screams of Mumu Sharah's harem as they came tumbling out of the gaming rooms, heading for the safety of the front doors.

It was, as Quist had predicted, every man for himself. No one seemed to pay any attention to anyone but himself. Quist was only a few feet from the man with the machine pistol. He took him from behind, delivering the same kind of lethal chopping blow that had polished off the man in the basement. The machine pistol slithered away across the marble floor. Quist recovered it. Still nobody seemed to have noticed him or paid any attention to what he was doing.

He stepped into the elevator and pressed the button for the ninth floor. He wasn't sure he would ever make it, the smoke was so thick, so overpowering. On the ninth floor he found himself down on his hands and knees, crawling for safety. The ninth floor fire alarm threatened to split his eardrums. The air was fresher, breathable, outside the elevator shaft. He wiped at his eyes which were smarting from the smoke. Then he saw Lydia, standing in the doorway to 9A. She came to him.

"Where are they?" he asked. He was ready for them now, armed with the machine pistol.

"They took off when the first alarm sounded," Lydia said. "My God, Julian, it seemed to take so long. I thought you hadn't made it."

"I made it."

He took her hand and pulled her down the hall to the fire stairs. He wasn't prepared to risk the smoke in the elevator shaft again. There were other people now, coming down from above, emerging from each floor on the way down. They were, Quist guessed, mostly staff people—maids from each floor, half-dressed men who had been wakened from their sleep. They were screaming and shouting at each other. It was a full-blown panic. Everyone pushed and shoved, trying to get past each other. Quist kept a steadying arm around Lydia to keep her from falling. You could be trampled to death if you lost your footing.

The lobby was bedlam when they reached it. People were charging toward the doors to the street and at the same time Quist saw that an army of people were forcing their way in from the outside, firemen, men who appeared to be wearing white armbands tied around their jacket sleeves. From outside came the wail of sirens from fire equipment. Eric Tranter, bless him, had been prepared.

Quist had fought his way almost to the doors when he ran head on into Dan Garvey, wearing one of the white armbands.

"Julian! Lydia!" Garvey called out.

"Get Lydia out of here," Quist said. "Get her out, and away, and stay with her."

"You?" Garvey said.

"Barney Steel is somewhere at the top of this funeral pyre," Quist said.

"I'll go with you," Garvey said.

"Get Lydia out of here and stay with her!" Quist shouted.

Then someone grabbed him from behind and spun him around.

"You're not going anywhere, Quist!" Colonel Slade, his face like a rock mask, was pointing a handgun straight at Lydia. "You sonofabitch, I warned you what would happen if you got into this act!"

Quist tried to maneuver in front of Slade to protect Lydia, but he was off balance, and some screaming women jostled him still further away. He heard a gun go off and turned, in despair, to look at Lydia. She was standing there, Garvey's arm around her. Slade was down on his hands and knees, blood pouring out of his mouth. Just behind Garvey was a girl in a pale blue linen suit, a white cloth tied around her arm, a gun held steadily, pointed at Slade. Sergeant Duane!

"White armbands mean friends," Garvey said. "Take someone with you, Julian. Don't try to be a hero!"

"Will I do?" someone asked at Quist's elbow.

He turned and saw his friend Lieutenant Kreevich.

Quist felt a great surge of hope. "Mark!"

"How do we get to Steel?" Kreevich asked.

"Go, Dan!" Quist said. He watched as Garvey got Lydia out the entrance doors and onto the street, and then he turned to Kreevich. Black clouds of smoke blurred the lieutenant's face. "I don't think we can risk the elevators," he said. "Not at this level. The shafts are like chimneys for the fire. The fire stairs."

"Twenty-three flights up?" Kreevich asked. "Brother!"

Clutching the machine pistol, Quist headed back for the fire stairs, Kreevich behind him. Fear for Lydia that had been eating at his heart was replaced by anger. Calloway and Company would already be doing something about Barney Steel. Would they just leave him to die of his own terror, or would they have other plans for him? There could be a couple of billion dollars at stake if the estimates of Steel's fortune were accurate. They would try to get him somewhere else and turn the screws. A psychotic Barney Steel would probably pay millions and millions of dollars for his miserable life.

Quist and Kreevich did pretty well, breasting the tide of escaping people in the enclosed fire stairs, for five or six flights, and then both men stopped to lean against the wall, gasping for breath. Then on and up—forever, Quist thought.

"Better take it easy than not make it at all," Kreevich muttered.

At the ninth or tenth floor—Quist had lost track—they went

out into a hallway to have a look at the elevator shafts. They pressed an up button and waited. A little needle over the elevator door showed them that the lifts were still working. A car was headed their way. But when the door slid open a cloud of stifling black smoke drove them back.

There was no choice but the fire stairs and they still weren't halfway to the penthouse. They climbed again, conserving what energy they could. The machine pistol he was carrying suddenly seemed to Quist to weigh a ton. He wanted to just sit down on the stairs and give up. But they kept on.

Finally—was it the same day—they came to the top, both men's bodies shaking from the effort, both men fighting to breathe. Quist found himself facing the door that had been opened to him in the past by unseen hands. There was no door handle.

"There's some kind of electronic eye here," Quist said.

"Screw electronic eyes," Kreevich said.

Both men put their shoulders to the door and tried to force it. It was like an immovable stone wall.

"Try shooting the lock out," Kreevich said.

Quist took a step backward and opened fire with the machine pistol. He had fired almost a complete round of ammunition when the door opened slowly, as if it had been pushed from the inside by some ghostly hand.

Beyond the door Steel's room was not believable. The heat that Barney Steel had had pumped through the air conditioning vents had brought smoke with it, all the way from the basement. It was like a thick, stinking London fog. Quist, the machine pistol at the ready, couldn't even see the scrim at the far end of the room behind which there had always been the man in the ski mask with the high-powered rifle. He took a few steps forward.

The Morris chair was empty.

Quist moved all the way to the scrim. No one there. No one in the john. Barney Steel had been removed.

"There's a second fire stair," Quist told Kreevich. "They told me—a way for Steel to get out without going through the hotel. It must be at the back somewhere."

"Please God, let it go down, not up," Kreevich said, and was seized by a fit of coughing.

Behind the scrim vacated by the man in the ski mask Quist found the second fire stair. Time was against them now. How quickly had these people managed to move Barney Steel? How able was Steel, operating under his own power, to negotiate twenty-three flights of stairs? Would they pull him out at some other floor and keep him hidden there? Quist told himself they would almost certainly try to get Steel out of the Palace and away. Not only was the building unsafe, but it was swarming with police and other law men. Calloway and the others must have to keep Barney Steel alive or they would have left him to suffocate in this room.

Quist and Kreevich started down the fire stairs. There were no people using this rear exit, probably built explicitly for Steel's use. There might not be exits to other floors, and as they moved downward Quist and Kreevich saw none.

Barney Steel was still in it—this private avenue. About halfway down they came on him. He was stretched out on the stone steps, wrapped in his filthy blue bathrobe, gasping for breath. The man in the ski mask was trying to get him up to his feet with Steel protesting feebly.

"No more, no further! I can't make it!"

Ski Mask had put his rifle down on the stone steps as he tried to lift Steel. He looked up and found himself looking into the muzzle of Kreevich's hand gun.

"Get the rifle," Kreevich said to Quist.

Quist moved, and Ski Mask attempted a desperate countermove. The two men went tumbling down the stairs together to the next landing. Quist, scrambling to his feet, found Ski Mask lying still beside him. A deep cut on the back of the man's head oozed blood.

Quist struggled back up to where Kreevich stood over a weeping, protesting Barney Steel. Steel clutched at Quist with his clawlike hands.

"For God sake help me! They are going to kill me."

"Someone's probably waiting for him at the end of the line," Kreevich said.

"We can't take him back upstairs. He couldn't survive in that room," Quist said. "Can you walk, Mr. Steel?"

Saliva drooled from the corners of the pale mouth. "No! No, I—I have no strength left."

It wasn't possible, but Quist somehow did it. He picked Steel up and held him in his arms. The wreck of a man seemed to weigh scarcely more than a small child.

They started down, Kreevich leading the way, Quist staggering a little under his burden. Steel seemed to be muttering prayers. Down they went, flight after flight. Kreevich had Quist's machine pistol along with his own gun. They were just a few steps above the street level when a door opened from the outside and the giant figure of His Excellency the President of Kambashi, wearing his British uniform, confronted them.

"Well, well, Mr. Quist, you really have become a public nuisance," Mumu Sharah said. For once he wasn't smiling.

"Out of the way," Kreevich said, leveling the machine pistol at the huge black man.

"You will not shoot me, Mr. Policeman," Mumu said. "It would create an international incident. I will take Barney, if you please." Two other men appeared in the doorway behind him. "Bring the car right alongside the door, gentlemen." He took a step up.

Barney Steel screamed. "Keep him away from me! Please, God, keep him away."

"International incidents don't concern me, Sharah," Kreevich said, quietly. "Just back down out of the way."

The wide white smile appeared. "You have to be joking, Mr. Policeman," Mumu Sharah said. A huge hand reached for his holstered gun.

Kreevich fired. He was an expert with weapons. He fired at Sharah's knee. The giant went down, a look of utter surprise on his face. Then he stood up. He couldn't walk on that shattered kneecap, but he did. Quist lowered Barney Steel to the stairs and shielded him with his own body.

Mumu Sharah was shouting now—shouting what were obvious obscenities in his native language. He was still tugging at his holster, having some difficulty with his gun. But he managed to get it out.

Kreevich opened fire with the machine pistol. This was no longer a delaying action. Quist thought the machine pistol would cut Sharah in half, but Mumu kept coming, a look of total disbelief on his face. He was firing his gun now, but wildly. He didn't have control of his reflexes any longer. Kreevich, his face gone deathly pale, kept firing. Mumu kept coming till just before he reached Kreevich, and then he went down actually grabbing at Kreevich's leg in a last convulsive gesture. Then he rolled over and lay staring with glassy, dead eyes at the ceiling.

"Believed he was immortal!" Kreevich said. "My God!"

He stepped over the body and reached the door. A black limousine was pulled up just outside with a man at the wheel. Kreevich covered the driver.

"Open the rear door," he ordered.

The other two men had taken cover somewhere beyond the door. Perhaps they had lost their nerve. Perhaps with Mumu gone they had no taste for murder. Kreevich turned his head.

"Get him in the car," he said to Quist.

"You're turning him over to them?"

"You're going with him," Kreevich said.

Quist was too stunned to do anything but what he was told. He carried Barney Steel to the car and lifted him into the plush interior. Kreevich handed him the machine pistol.

"If the driver gives you any trouble, chum, blow his head off," Kreevich said.

Quist got in beside the groaning Barney Steel. "Drive," he said.

"Where to, sir?" the man at the wheel asked.

"How the hell do I know? Just drive!" Quist said.

As the car swerved away Quist looked back at the building. Black smoke was pouring out of windows almost to the top. Presently the Steel Palace would be no more.

Quist lay stretched out in a wicker deck chair on the terrace of his Beekman Place apartment in New York. He was wearing pale tan slacks, a bright orange sports shirt, and sandals on his feet.

"I may never leave this spot—today, tomorrow, next week, or next month," he said.

Lydia sat on a wicker stool beside him, wearing a light green kaftan. There were ice-cooled drinks. There were two guests, Eric Tranter and Lieutenant Kreevich.

"I have been received with more enthusiasm in my time," Kreevich said, grinning.

"All I want is to be alone with Lydia, aware that my rooms aren't bugged, that there are no gunmen outside the doors—that my liquor cabinet is full," Quist said.

"But there are things you need to be caught up on, Julian," Tranter said. "In the first place the Steel Palace is the charred skeleton of a building. Total loss."

"A fifty-two-million-dollar bonfire," Kreevich said. "And do you know something? Barney Steel is already talking about building another fifty-million-dollar jail for himself."

"Steel is all right?" Lydia asked.

"He's in the Walter Reed Hospital in Washington, surrounded by police, FBI, CIA, Secret Service. For all I know the President himself may be riding shotgun," Tranter said.

"Francine?" Quist asked.

"In the same hospital," Tranter said, "talking her little heart out to the CIA. Mumu Sharah and Colonel Slade are dead, both shot by police officers. Calloway and Yeager and Freddy Lenz seemed to have gotten away in the wild confusion. Maybe they got to Kambashi as originally planned, but who will protect them when they get there? Half a dozen of Mumu's enemies are in a struggle to take over power. Kambashi is not a healthy place for Mumu's friends and allies. Foster Martin, the American expert, has copped a plea. He is telling all to get off on a minor charge of conspiracy."

"What is all?" Quist asked.

Tranter shrugged. "The Big Five, you called them—the Big Five had come to the conclusion that Barney Steel was close to the end of his road. They had served him for years, helping to amass an Arabian Nights' fortune and unbelievable power. They thought that when Steel died all this would be divided among them. Steel had no family, no wives, or ex-wives, no children. Who else would he leave it all to but his loyal friends? And then there was some kind of disagreement and Steel showed them his will." Tranter shook his head. "Would you believe that everything he possesses—oil wells, railroads, airlines, hotels, copper mines, diamond mines—God knows what else—is to be liquidated and the lump sum in cash to be divided among three women who once gave him pleasure in bed? They had provided him with the only love and tenderness he had ever known."

"Oh brother," Quist said.

"One is a nightclub singer," Tranter said, "one is a successful madam in Acapulco, and one a lady novelist who lives on an island off the coast of Spain. The will is irrevocable. Steel fixed it so he couldn't change it himself. When the Big Five saw how the land lay, they dreamed up a way to get rich anyhow. They used Steel's fear of violent death to force him to help them. The invitations—the grand opening—and then the rip-off." Tranter smiled at Quist. "If you weren't such a nosy bastard, the whole thing might have worked."

"You do know that you could spend the next twenty years in jail as an arsonist, don't you, Julian?" Kreevich asked. "But cheer up. Nobody can prove anything if they wanted to, and I don't know of anyone who wants to. Steel tells Tranter he would like to reward you in some fashion for getting him out to safety."

"There is one thing he could do," Quist said. He smiled. "He could get the Motion Picture Academy of Arts and Sciences to award Lydia a special Oscar. Her performance as a heart-attack victim would put most Hollywood stars to shame." He covered Lydia's hand with his. "And now, chums, it seems as if it has been a long time since Lydia and I have been together without someone listening. If you don't mind—?"